Praise for

The Coin

"Zaher draws a Venn diagram of the glamorously neurotic and the politically oppressed, then sets her protagonist spinning in that maddening little overlap." —*Vulture*

"A very stylish novel that manages to broach class and stateless-ness with tact and humor, while also touching on beauty, sex, love and the nature of civilization itself, all from a Palestinian debut novelist." —*Literary Hub*

"*The Coin* is a filthy, elegant book, keen on the fixations that over-take the body and upend a life."
—RAVEN LEILANI, author of *Luster*

"I loved this bonkers novel. I was hooked by the voice and mes-merized by the glamorous and sordid hijinks. I have never read such a strange and recognizable representation of post-2016 New York City, its luxury and squalor. Zaher is a writer to watch."
—ELIF BATUMAN, author of *Either/Or* and *The Idiot*

"*The Coin* is a taut, caustic wonder. Like Jean Rhys, Yasmin Zaher captures the outrageous loneliness of contemporary life, the gradual and total displacement of the human heart. This is a novel of wealth, filth, beauty, and grief told in clarion prose and with unbearable suspense. I was in its clutches from the first page." —HILARY LEICHTER, author of
Terrace Story and *Temporary*

"*The Coin* does much more than meet the highest standards of literature: it sets its own standards. It combines intimate bodily observations and repetitive daily routines with delicate power plays, displays of crumbling authority, and interrogations of justice, all against the background of global violence. And should we really be surprised that it was a young Palestinian citizen of Israel who performed this miracle? Those who dismiss Palestinians as the violent Other of the Western civilization will discover that a Palestinian can see the truth of our messy world better than we ourselves. *The Coin* is not a wonderful beginning that promises masterpieces to come—it already *is* a masterpiece."

—SLAVOJ ŽIŽEK

"Yasmin Zaher must have used electric ink to write this book. It is charged with such strangeness and humor; it glows with disobedience. A marvelous novel." —AYŞEGÜL SAVAŞ, author of *White on White* and *Walking on the Ceiling*

"*The Coin* is a brilliant, audacious powerhouse of a novel. A story of obsession and appetite, politics and class, it is deliciously unruly. An exceptional debut by an outrageous new talent."
—KATIE KITAMURA, author of *Intimacies* and *A Separation*

"*The Coin* is marvelous, absolutely mental, and full of pleasurable surprises. I read it in a flash. What an entrance."
—ISABELLA HAMMAD, author of *Enter Ghost* and *The Parisian*

THE COIN

THE
COIN

A NOVEL

Yasmin Zaher

CATAPULT  NEW YORK

I would like to thank Monika Woods and Kendall Storey,
without whom this book wouldn't exist.

THE COIN

First Catapult edition: 2024

ISBN: 978-1-64622-210-0

Library of Congress Control Number: 2024933701

Jacket design by Jaya Miceli
Jacket art for Malone Souliers AW21 campaign by Isabelle Wenzel
Book design by Olenka Burgess

Catapult
New York, NY
books.catapult.co

Printed in the United States of America

10 9 8 7 6 5 4 3 2 1

THE COIN

Dirt was my first hypothesis. It had its way of going where nothing else would go, and I kept seeing it, on surfaces, in corners, underneath furniture and long nails. I always noticed it, which is not unusual, because I noticed many things, beautiful things too. I saw colors, birds moving in trees. I had been gifted with the pleasure of all of these, together with my suffering of all of these, and especially the dirt. Everywhere. And in New York, so much of it. Stubborn and full of the promise of disease.

I had just moved to America, and I was working as a teacher at a middle school. It was never something I wanted to do, I would have preferred a job with glamour and prestige, but it was a job I enjoyed. I've always been motivated by pleasure, never by money, because money I had enough of and pleasure one cannot possess. And teachers have power, don't forget that.

Franklin had blue walls, blue stairs, blue doors. All the boys there grew up in blue bedrooms, I imagined. Anywhere else, that blue would have been sickening, but at a school I found it joyous. It reminded me of my vacation to Havana with Sasha, how the shops there only displayed the basic products. Bread, eggs, soap, toilet paper. Basic blue. Now that I think of it, the Franklin blue was the blue of the Cuban flag.

You're right that the American flag also features the color blue, but one cannot get to the bottom of it with all those stripes and stars. What an overbearing flag, just the thought of it twists my eyeballs.

At the end of our trip to Cuba, Sasha said to me, very directly, I know that you need to get out of there, I'm going to help you. He got me the job through a colleague who was friends with Aisha, the headmistress. It was a win-win, because I got to leave Palestine, and Sasha got me, and Franklin got a donation from Sasha.

I was hired halfway through September. It was early enough in the year and as Aisha told me, it was time for change. When she walked me into the classroom and I saw all the copies of *Moby-Dick*, my first thought was that I was in way over my head, that this was a terrible idea. I had never read any of the books in that closet, never read Twain, never heard of Brontë. But the first weeks went by and I realized that as long as the boys scored high enough on the standardized tests, I could do whatever I wanted with them. And that's when I began to see myself as really big and important.

No, not as their savior, much more than that. Their general.

The boys were living at an important moment. Very soon they were going to get dirty in the streets of New York. But for the time being they were still clean, and I liked being around them.

I have to be totally honest with you. We're going to get somewhere good. You will see that I'm a moral woman, that all I want is to be clean.

I wore a very nice perfume then, Lys Méditer-anée by Edouard Fléchier, very strong and sexual. I always imagined it smelled like an inseminated flower on a summer night in a coastal city. It smelled like the opposite of incest, like a just-conceived superspecies.

The Lys was useful to me, living in a big city like New York. When I moved there, not yet old, I was a free woman. I thought there was no better feeling in this world than leaving work to walk along a Manhattan avenue, wearing a violent perfume with no one waiting for you at home. I had done the math and come to the right answer, which is always zero, or even less. To love is not worth it. The benefits, whatever they are, are mostly a comfort from the relentless emptiness of being human, a separate being alone in the world. They are not worth putting yourself at the mercy of others. This isn't a secret, I said this to people, I even said it to my students. To love is to be taken hostage, boys, it's Stockholm syndrome.

Yes, I was with Sasha, we had been together for years, but he didn't have any power over me. I never thought of him when he wasn't there, my heart never skipped a beat. I'm not proud of this, I would have preferred a relationship of passion, but I always need one foot on the ground.

Looking back now, that time in New York feels like a dream. When you're inside a dream, everything makes sense. But when you wake up, the shapes lose their solidity and the logic is strange. So I have to tell you quickly, before I forget.

In the morning I brushed my teeth with a soft toothbrush and my favorite Cattier toothpaste. Then I washed my face with an oil-based cleanser, followed by a water-based cleanser, followed by toner. All imported from Korea, the world capital of skin like porcelain, purity, and nothingness. Two thousand more years of snail cream and you will see a woman's brain through her face. Then, after drinking a glass of hot lemon water, a glass of lukewarm water, and a cup of coffee, I emptied my bowels. This happened easily, gloriously, requiring no effort or thought, like flipping through an abridged history of the fall of an empire. All out, insides clean.

After work I got in the shower and repeated the steps of the skin-care regimen under the hot water. I washed my hair with two kinds of shampoo, I scrubbed my feet with a pumice stone, I cleaned my ears and underneath my nails with cotton buds. Slippers from the shower to the bedroom. Ready for the white sheets. I never, ever got into bed without showering.

I was a clean woman then, you could say. In cleanliness, I invested money, time, attention. But it was not enough. The dirt kept piling, pain is an accumulation.

The boys at Franklin had gotten the opportunity to attend an excellent school. They didn't need to pay for it, it was their ticket to social mobility. So they had to dress accordingly, speak accordingly, read accordingly. They were required to wear khakis, a button-down shirt, a jacket, and dress shoes. The uniform wasn't strict, they could play around with it, it was America after all. The point was that these boys were meant to dress for the class that they were going to ascend to. They always looked dashing, the outfit cast them in a kind of performance. They rarely fought or said crude things, they were polite and charming. Like domesticated animals.

I could tell, early on, which boys had style. Sal, for instance, showed up on my first day of school wearing all mustard and a checkered bowtie. I observed his wardrobe throughout the week, admiring his mother for her dedication, his clothes always pressed. Jay was simple but dignified, although he sometimes neglected to tuck in his shirt after going to the bathroom, unlike Leonard, who was my star student and always tucked in his shirt tightly, his baby belly held firmly above a brown leather belt, I assumed his father's.

Myself, I had already arrived and I didn't need to earn

anything. I dressed the way I dressed, the way I saw myself. Never like a WASP, you would never see me in pastels or pearls or a pencil skirt. I did carry a Birkin, though, I had inherited it from my mother. It was black, made from baby bull leather, and it was surprisingly utilitarian. It fit the standard A4 page and had two pockets inside, one for my wallet and phone, the other for my MetroCard. And it had feet. Yes, feet. Four studs on its underbelly that kept it upright and clean, even when sitting on a subway seat. This bag was self-sufficient, it took care of itself.

I had carried this bag for years and no one had noticed it, but in New York, it was turning heads. Women of all ages looked at me, even little girls and some gay guys looked at me, especially when I was uptown, turning the corner of Madison into a ray of sunlight. As you can imagine, this was quite a revelation. You see, I came from a place where a bag could never have power, where only violence spoke. And suddenly I had something that others wanted to possess, I was a woman who others wanted to embody.

Well, it was just a bag, let's not exaggerate. But sometimes the smallest detail is a portal into another world.

I t's strange where we start stories. I might as well have started from my birth if I was going to be proper and methodical. But the dirt is not a metaphor, I really saw it. In my ear canals, inside my nose, around my ankles. Do I disgust you? I don't look dirty, do I?

One day, I began to notice that my body was dirtier than usual. It was a pleasant day, in late September, and I went for a long walk after Franklin, wandering down some streets that were neither numbered nor lettered. I wasn't afraid of being lost, there was always a cab around the corner, and when I felt that I'd had enough, the sun was setting, I raised my hand in the air and a taxi took me home. I entered my apartment and decided to take a shower. I did this naturally and with no intentions, I was only doing what felt good.

Before I got in the water, I remembered that I had a Turkish hammam loofah in my suitcase. I brought it out, stepped into the shower, slipped my hand inside the loofah, and began scrubbing. The bathroom was small, the bathtub short.

First, my right hand scrubbed my left arm. It burned. The water was hot, my heart began to race and it gave me the energy to continue. As I said, it was a pleasant day and perhaps in my boredom I had found a way to make it exciting. I closed my eyes and rubbed as hard and fast as I could, until my muscle began to stiffen, which wasn't long, I'd be exaggerating if I said it took more than thirty seconds. As you can see, I'm a small woman, I wait for others to open doors for me.

When I opened my eyes, I saw the miniature gray snakes. They fell to my feet, three or four of them.

I looked at them and immediately I knew. I mean, I had seen them before, but not like this. A heart-faced woman had once scrubbed me in a Turkish hammam and I saw them there too, wiggling in the splash on marble. But the snakes of New York were scary and ghoulish, like my own voice in the mouth of a total stranger.

I took the dirt to heart. I knew that the snakes were not just a material fact but that they were a sign of something very bad, something terrifying that was happening to my body.

The loofah was a harmless-looking thing that in reality was wicked and rough. I continued, scrubbing my entire body, peeling off the dead skin. I told myself that this was a death that I could manage, if only I worked hard enough, if I stayed clean and organized. But I had no stamina, and when I switched, left to right, I did not see any snakes. My left side is not as strong. And you will see, as I proceed, that this is a condition of asymmetry. The left is cleaner, but it is weak. The right is strong and covered in filth.

The snakes lay there in the bathtub. I bent over, picked them up, and threw them all in the small garbage can in the bathroom. I didn't like the sight of them, just lying there, so I dug my hand inside the garbage and stirred it, flipping them as one flips a tender risotto.

I got out of the shower and tiptoed back to my bedroom. It must have been dark out, yes, I remember it was. I wouldn't have done it otherwise. I didn't have a problem with my neighbors seeing me naked from the bedroom window, but the kitchen window faces Fulton Street, and I didn't walk naked by that window at night. It's a good area, a great location. But how do I say it? Working class, going to and from work, always tired, and I didn't want to be seen by them.

I'm just going to say it. I didn't want poor people to see my body. Their desperation scared me.

That evening, I went to dinner at Sasha's. He also lived in the neighborhood. Do you know the tall clock tower, the one that looks like a dick? Sasha was in real estate and a few years back he had even bought the small building across from Kushner's 666, which, by my advice, he later leased to Salvatore Ferragamo. But Sasha was very humble about it. When people asked him he said he was in real estate, and you wouldn't know, he could have been just another Eastern European broker.

I wore a dress by McQueen, my arms and legs were like polished bronze, but underneath my dress everything else was dirty, beginning to rot.

I couldn't sleep at Sasha's. All night I thought about my dirty body and the place I could not clean. It was behind me, between my shoulder blades, the only part of my body I could not touch, nor fully see, the part of my body which must have been the dirtiest, because I couldn't get to it with the Turkish hammam loofah.

left Sasha's apartment early in the morning. We lived only three blocks apart, in the heart of Brooklyn, where all the subway lines cross. He was the reason I moved there, I chose that apartment because I wanted to be close to him, not in a dependent way, but in the way it's nice to live near a convenience store.

There was a small park between us, on the intersection of Fulton, Ashland, and Lafayette. It was shaped like a triangle and I had to walk around it, because there was no gate to enter, no way to cut across. I suspected because they didn't want homeless people sleeping in there. I imagined that one day in the not-too-distant future, when there were no more poor people in the neighborhood, there would be a grand opening of the locked park. Or perhaps they would build a high-rise there, something like the London Shard, but they would name it after some surgical tool in homage to having defeated the cancer.

As soon as I entered my apartment, I took off my dress, it smelled like my perfume and lamb fat, and stood in front of the living room mirror, a tube of toothpaste in hand.

As I mentioned, the toothpaste was by Cattier, it's a French brand. I believe it's the best toothpaste on the market. Creamy and matte, perfect for painting on skin. I was going to test my new hypothesis, I wanted to see if there was a place I could not touch.

I dabbed a bit of toothpaste on my index finger and reached my arm behind my head to draw a line on my back. I then twisted my arm from underneath itself and drew another line from below. Then more toothpaste, in vertical lines behind my shoulders. The result was an asymmetrical square in the center of my back, the area of my limitations.

Of course, I wanted to know more. I emptied half the tube in my hands and tried, as hard as I could, to paint inside the square. I wrestled myself, as if I were in a straitjacket. I then painted my lower back, my shoulders, my arms, my underarms, and my ass cheeks. I painted my feet, my legs, and I had such big calves, city calves, from all the walking. Peasants too have large calves, but theirs are matched by thick wrists, whereas mine were delicate like the collected stems of a bouquet of flowers. I told you already, this is a condition of asymmetry.

I even used a hand mirror for better views, the type women use to be stunned by their vaginas. I had succeeded in painting my entire body, except for that square at the center of my back.

Yes, it was the part of my body that must have been the dirtiest.

I washed off the Cattier and spread out my blue yoga mat on the bedroom floor. I didn't do any yoga, I just lay down, admitting to myself that something wasn't right. My body didn't feel right, because to feel good, casually, is to not feel your body.

I lasted eight months in New York, less than a child lasts in his mother's belly. It's a lot if you think about it, it's enough to make a human. I'm telling you this story as a reminder to myself, as a promise for the future. It's a promise that nothing lasts, not even you, not even us. No two separate things can be linked forever.

Because of all the time I spent cleaning, I often had to improvise in the classroom. When I felt that there was trust between us, that the students weren't going to tell on me, I introduced the concept of a free class. It must have been October already. It was a Friday and I was tired from the week, I hadn't prepared a lesson plan, I even showed up a few minutes after the morning bell.

The sixth graders were my first class of the day, and they were the most pliable. They had just started at Franklin and it was all so novel and exciting for them, you would think that they were entering Hogwarts. I said to them, In the next hour we will imagine that we're free. If you want to read, read. If you want to play games on your phone, play games on your phone. If you want to sleep, sleep. Several of them did sleep, because even at the age of twelve they were overworked and tired.

With the seventh graders, I improvised and taught them something from the eighth-grade syllabus. I said, You have been doing exceptionally well and I'm impressed by your level of maturity, so today I will give you something much more advanced, material from the eighth-grade syllabus. The boys were anxious, worried that it would be too difficult and they would get a bad grade. No, I said, this is a free class. You will not be tested and there will be no homework. After that, I wasted ten minutes fiddling with the projector and then showed them the first thirty minutes of *Scent of a Woman*.

The room was dark, the boys were not yet hormonal and their skin was smooth, reflecting the cold light of the projector. Most of my students were Black, and the rest were immigrants. Sure, they saw themselves in ads, but mostly on the subway, rarely on billboards. They looked like the kids in the posters for community college, corporate welfare, the occasional fashion house or beauty product blending the boys' tones for a trendier image. They were on the margins, and I understand the drive to reclaim American democracy for all, but I think it's an afterthought. I knew that life was already hard for them and would likely only get harder. Life was hard for me too at that age. I wasn't poor like them, but I didn't see myself on billboards either, to say the least. When I started the job, Aisha had told me that two of my seventh graders were Dreamers. I wanted to talk to them about it but I felt incompetent. I didn't know any Latinos, which is to say that I'd never been in the home of one.

While we watched the film, I felt my chest tightening, like it was keeping something from escaping from within me. I wasn't feeling well, I thought that my body was trying to tell me something. During lunchtime, I didn't sit with the rest of the teachers. I shut myself in the tiny staff bathroom, spread my Burberry trench coat on the floor, lay down on it, and propped my feet on the sink. I remained like this for the entire break, trying to listen, ignoring any knocks or attempts to open the door.

I absorbed many smells in there, and they stayed with me for days. But at the end of that hour, I was full of determination and resolve. I realized that if no one could stop me from lying down on the bathroom floor, then I could do so much more at Franklin. The bell rang and I marched up the stairs and entered my classroom. The eighth graders were very bright, hardworking, and full of ideas. I gave them their first assignment, to write about an encounter with a stranger. They began to panic, of course. So many of them had performance anxiety, they had already been conditioned to please, and they wanted to know what I expected of them. I'll explain, I said, let me share a little story with you. I assumed a confident position, sitting on the teacher's desk with my knees slightly parted, my hands on the table behind me. During lunch today, I said, I saw an old woman slip and fall down the steps of Presto on Eighth Street. It wasn't serious, but she was a nice old lady and she hurt her elbow. The barista and I helped her up and got her into a taxi. She needed to rest, the poor lady. Then, and I'm not kidding, boys, as soon as the taxi drove away, I saw another person fall down the same steps of Presto. He was a young man, and I think he was a little drunk.

I stood up from the teachers' desk and imitated a drunkard's walk, wobbling around the classroom, bumping into the students' desks, which made them laugh. Do you know what I did, boys? I walked right past him, I didn't even blink. But now I can't stop thinking about it. Help me with this, why did I help one stranger but not the other?

I looked around at them, they were confused. There is no right or wrong answer, boys, I'm just thinking out loud. We can just have a free discussion for a few minutes, this is a free class.

Jay spoke first. When the class was quiet, he was always the one who came to my rescue. He said that maybe I was scared of the drunk man. He said that in his building there's an alcoholic, that's the word he used, and sometimes he finds him sleeping inside the elevator. He is too scared to ride with him, so he has to climb the stairs to the seventh floor.

Very well, Jay, don't take the elevator with the alcoholic. Small spaces are contagious and you could get drunk off his breath, I said. And maybe, maybe that's why I didn't want to help the man outside. Imagine I came in here drunk, and gave it to you. Jay nodded, and I told him to write his composition about the alcoholic. Then I went around the classroom, one by one, and helped them find something to write about.

While it was quiet, my body woke up again. It brought tears to my eyes, and I had to hide them by ducking underneath the desk to fetch random items out of my bag. I wanted to leave the students there and go back to the staff bathroom, to listen again, but I couldn't do that, it would have been chaos. I told them that just one page of writing would suffice, and they could go home as soon as they'd finished.

They looked around, complained of bigger handwriting, smaller notebooks. So you have two options, I said, either you write two hundred words or you can write as little as you want but I'll count it for your final grade. They all began counting out loud and confusing one another. Minutes later, the notebooks were piled on my desk. By the time the bell rang the classroom had been tidied and the whiteboard erased. It was my last class of the day. I left quickly and took the students' notebooks with me, stuffing them in my Birkin. Before I entered the subway I stopped at a 7-Eleven, bought a painkiller, and swallowed it dry. On the train, I sat the heavy bag on the yellow seat and waited for the pill to kick in.

By the time I got to my neighborhood, I was doing considerably better. The sky was clear, and a gentle wind was pushing off the first leaves of fall. I could still smell the staff bathroom on my trench coat though, it smelled like skunkweed and yeast. I took it off and looked at it. It was a marvelous creation, creamy and delicate. I had worn it for years and it had been so loyal to me, so sturdy, so enduringly stylish. I took my lipstick from the pocket and left my trench coat there, on top of the orange bin intended for paper recycling. It was too dirty for me to keep, but I imagined it wasn't too dirty for a stranger.

I entered my apartment and dropped the students' notebooks on the dining table. It was fifty square meters in a brick building, recently renovated with a skylight. I had a bed, a dining table, an armchair, and some lamps and mirrors. I didn't own a lot of things, but a lot could go wrong. I could see a matte layer of dust on the kitchen counter, that there was a knot in the cord of the table lamp, that the spice jars were misaligned. It was also very noisy, crisscrossed by the evening rush. I told you already, Fort Greene is a transit neighborhood. There was the B67 exhaling loudly at the bus stop, like a beast in heat. The music blaring from the black Toyotas with open windows. The loitering outside the smoke shop, the ambulances, the demonic ticking of the stoplight, the swooshing of the trees in the park across the street, and their movement, too, which I could see through the dirty glass of the kitchen windows.

So I did what I had to do. I began to throw things away, organize, and clean. This became a way of life. I could have paid someone to do it for me, the cleaning, but I couldn't trust another woman with my home, I was afraid that she would throw out an important scrap of paper. It sounds dramatic, but I became a clean freak. It's a common condition, and one that isn't socially frowned upon. On the contrary, it's an indication of good character. When you walk into a woman's house and it's sparkling clean, you never think of all the madness entailed. You just praise her and maybe feel a hint of jealousy. You never think about all the years she spent on her knees, breaking nails and huffing Mr Muscle.

To be honest with you, in New York I saw the dirtiest people I had ever seen, although I'd never been to a third-world country. I came from Palestine, which was neither a country nor the third world, it was its own thing, and the women in my family placed a lot of importance on being clean, perhaps because there was little else they could control in their lives.

But in New York, people didn't care for cleanliness. In the street, I saw dead rats, diapers, toothpicks, and drug baggies. I saw bottles of mascara and tampons, proof that the women, too, were dirty. New Yorkers could walk by a splatter of diarrhea on the subway tiles, bagel and coffee in hand, and not think twice. They would still live there tomorrow in the greatest city on earth. The city embraced the dirt like it was an aesthetic. Rust and bricks, black trash bags lining the trenches, millions of pieces of gum on the sidewalks like polka dots by Yayoi Kusama.

But I couldn't embrace it. Gradually, I started wearing gloves on the subway, I hemmed all my pants so they wouldn't touch the ground. Half the day I held my breath.

That evening in October, I did it all, I stayed up until two in the morning. I cleaned the bathroom, the fridge, the closets, and all the corners, of all sizes, of which there were many. I even got to some tasks that had been looming over me for weeks. When I say this, something in particular comes to mind, a small scribble in red pencil or crayon. It was on the door frame of the bedroom, made by either a builder or a child. As I scrubbed at it, I heard a sound coming from my neighbor's apartment. A musical instrument. It took me a few seconds to recognize that it was a clarinet. I imagined the player was a man, because I'm always ready to fuck. The red scribble didn't come off, no matter how hard I tried. I despised it. It was a reminder that people had been there before me.

The next morning, I woke up with a stiff neck. It felt as if I had slept on a coin, a small and dense one, like a thick shekel or an old British pound, and in my dreams, it left an imprint of the queen.

When I was little, we took vacations in the South. One year, we were driving down the desert highway, myself, my mother, father, and brother in the car. It was a long ride, five hours or so, and I was playing with one shekel and twenty agoras, throwing them in the air and laughing. The shekel was a cute little silver, the agoras a pair of dumb golds. At some point, the shekel dropped from my hand, into my mouth, and disappeared. There was only the movement of the coin, and then nothing. I was a magician, but I had no training, just a scientist mother and a scientist father and a brother who was too old to bathe with me. You swallowed it, they all insisted. But the coin never again manifested, not as discomfort in my esophagus, nor as constipation, the little coin did not block my little anus, and there was no shine to my poop after the full day at the pool. There was no metallic burping at the breakfast buffet, nor the flavor of a beggar's finger in my mouth. Why is it that the poor are dirty and the rich are clean?

As I said, it's strange where we start stories. I could have started here instead. On our drive back from the South, on the desert highway again, my father fell asleep at the wheel. My parents both died, and my brother and I survived.

It was a tragedy, but somehow I got lucky, I was redeemed by a good inheritance. If anyone can understand this, I know it's you.

I wrote to my brother and explained to him that in New York I needed extra money each month, that I needed a cleaner, a cook, a masseur, an acupuncturist, a reiki healer, and a psychoanalyst. Maybe two or three cleaners, or one who is as serious as I am, although she would never have become a cleaner, there are not enough hours in the day to clean two homes with such rigor and commitment.

It was paper mail, but the answer came quickly, in a yellow envelope. I read it just once, walking up the stairs to my apartment. There is nothing I can do, he wrote, I intend to respect the will of our father. The will stipulated that I would get a strict allowance each month, and I would have no access to the estate beyond that. I could go get the will right now and read it word by word, but the thing always makes me sick to my stomach.

I had no choice but to obey my father's wishes. I owned the

rights to half of his estate. At the time of his death, about twenty-eight million seven hundred and fifty-five thousand US dollars. Control of the estate was strictly in the hands of the lawyer, then my brother. I had so much money, and no access to it. Sasha said I was simultaneously rich and poor.

My mother's wish was different. She wanted me to go to America. Many people have been able to make lives for themselves there, like Sasha, and even prosper. But my family's case was different. We kept trying and failing to emigrate, some said that we were cursed. It started with my grandmother's eldest sister, who was shipped to New York from Haifa and returned just three years later. Next was my grandmother, who was happy there, she said, but had to return to marry my grandfather. Then there was my mother, who doesn't know why she left America, she just did, life happened. And with me, it was the knowledge of all those women who had tried before me, of this momentum for failure, and it was also the political moment, the times had changed. America looked gloomier to me than in the pictures. There were crackheads in the streets and cokeheads in the high-rises. And there was what America had done abroad, in Vietnam, in Guatemala, and especially to my people. That makes sense, doesn't it? I mean, how could the devil be the dream?

That week, I showed the eighth graders a black-and-white video of Stokely Carmichael. A few weeks had gone by and I realized that truly nobody was supervising me at Franklin. Aisha never asked me what we were learning, there were no inspectors sent by the government, and I'd never seen a parent at school. I decided that instead of following the syllabus, I could make up my own, and I started with Stokely Carmichael.

When the students saw me walking into the classroom with the projector they got excited, they thought we were going to watch a movie. I didn't provide an introduction, I just started playing the video, and it was very short, so we watched it again and again.

It started with Stokely sitting on the couch with his mother. The mother has relaxed hair cut in a sweet bob, and a delicate scarf is tied around her neck. She is polite, too polite, or maybe the perfect amount. Stokely takes the mic and begins to interview his own mother. He asks her how many people live in their house and makes her count to eight. He asks her to describe their neighborhood. On the run-down side, she says, and she adds, The streets were dirty, garbage pails all flown around and not covered. It takes a while, but he makes her admit that they are poor because they are Black.

When the mother finally uttered the word *negro,* Jay gasped and covered his mouth with his hand. There was a long moment of silence, and I felt that time had stopped, which it never does with fourteen-year-olds. The classroom reeked of sulfur, I think one of the boys had egg salad in his backpack, so I opened a window.

The fourth or fifth time we watched the video, some of the boys stopped breathing, and my stomach began to hurt. I kept thinking, It's a good thing I'm good, or I could do some real damage here.

For their next writing composition, I assigned them to clandestinely interview a member of their household, to lead them to some truth that they refuse to acknowledge. For example, I said to them, I'm going to interview my brother about how much money he spends every week on the lottery. This was a lie, of course. My brother was in a different country and, as far as I knew, did not gamble. But I often lied to the boys, I did what I had to do to get the message across. I told them to manipulate and I really used that word. It sounds sinister but manipulation was not new to them. They were exposed to all sorts of things, some of them even watched porn.

I told them to do the interview at home and that we would write it up next week in class. I didn't want their families to see what they were learning, so I started collecting all of their notebooks at the end of each day. They were happy to leave the notebooks with me, to not have any homework. Try to remember the details of the interview, I told them. But if you forget a quote it's not a big deal, you can make it up, newspapers do it all the time.

J ay stayed behind, helping me clean the classroom. He was a gentle boy, naive, not very bright. He had trouble even understanding the assignments, somehow he always found a way to execute them in the wrong manner. But he was sweet, and he understood that he could save his grades by being loved, and when he helped me I knew he really meant it, because I saw him cleaning from the bottom of his heart, wanting to satisfy me in earnest, not just trying to get it over with like the other boys. I tasked him with the vacuuming and wiping. His doing the simple tasks freed me up to specialization. I did the corners of the room, the bookshelves, the radiator.

It didn't ever get clean. It was an old building, an old classroom with ugly blue carpeting.

After all the boys left and it was just the two of us, I told him to correct his posture. Jay wasn't growing properly and according to him he was the shortest kid in school, even shorter than the sixth graders. You have to always look presentable, Jay. Especially as a young Black man. People are racist, you know. But they are also stupid, as I always tell you boys. It's not hard to fool them, and if you look good they will automatically assume that you are more respectable. I told him that learning to be clean and looking presentable was part of his Franklin education. And I taught him that being tidy was important too, and also, I said, It's important to not own too many things, because once you do, you naturally become messier. What does your room look like? I asked. He said that his side was tidy but that his older brother was very messy. A pig, I snorted. They shared a room and a desk, but his brother never studied. You know, I told him, I used to share a room with my brother, and we put up a bedsheet between us, so that we could change our clothes freely, but also for the mental distance. You could give it a try, I said, that way when you sit down to study, you won't be distracted by his clutter, your mind will be clear.

Jay told me that he wanted to go to boarding school after Franklin, that he wanted to get out. He was a very sensitive boy, always needing support, and the thought of him fending for himself worried me. But still, I encouraged him. That's not a bad idea, I said. Sometimes we have to become independent of our families, not because we don't love them but because they weigh us down. My comment made him emotional, I felt that he wanted to cry. I changed the subject. You want to hear my secret to success, Jay? I have very few belongings, I'm focused on myself, I am my own greatest asset. And you, too, you are smart, kind, handsome. You are your own greatest asset, Jay. You don't need anything or anyone else.

On Saturday, I texted Sasha good morning and by nine we were sitting at The Academy. It was raining, and I didn't have my trench coat anymore, but the diner was just down the street, so I walked there quickly with my hands covering my hair.

I was glad to see Sasha early in the day. I was lively that morning, very funny and sharp. I told him about the new job, about my students. I bet you were a smart kid, I bet your teachers adored you, I said to him. I ordered an oatmeal and barely touched it because I was talking so much. He ordered a greasy plate of everything greasy and a chocolate milkshake. Do you want some? he asked, pushing the milkshake toward me. I told him I had decided to become vegan, that it was the best thing ever, and I whispered to him, It's like an anal orgasm first thing in the morning. He blushed and spilled some chocolate on his black T-shirt, which I could see was already dirty, there was a whitish stain by the collar and dandruff on his shoulders. Sasha had a hard time taking care of himself, in that material way, his mind was always elsewhere. He wiped the chocolate with his hand, and I thought, He still likes me, and I still possess him.

Sasha was the last remaining man in my life, but I had no sexual desire for him. I should have let him go, but I couldn't, because

I would have been left with nothing. I was still masturbating, thankfully, but it wasn't the same anymore. I didn't know who to think of and my EGR Game was barely working. I used to start with E, the hearty dinners, undressing politely, then the foreplay with G, he was always very good at that, he did a magic trick with his fingers. Then R for the passion, the long gazes and vigorous penetration, then back to E if I wanted to orgasm. It was an excellent strategy but it just wasn't working anymore, I couldn't hold them in my mind, I could hardly see their faces.

I ate a bit of my oatmeal then told Sasha, There is something in my body. He asked me what it was, I said that my body was dirty, my skin was shedding a lot, and there was a spot which I could not clean, between my shoulder blades. He looked at me, squinting, then took a long sip of his milkshake. He suggested that I come home with him and he'd give me a massage but I declined, knowing that after the massage he was going to slip his fingers inside me. That in itself was not the problem, the problem was that afterward he was going to lie next to me and sigh a big pathetic sigh and expect something in return. No, I couldn't do it. I'd rather get the massage from a stranger, and pay for it. As you know, money simplifies everything.

So do you want to go to a doctor? he asked. No, I answered, I'm sure if I go there they'll give me a painkiller and charge me a thousand dollars. Or they'll tell me I have cancer and I'm going to die and charge me a hundred thousand dollars just to make sure. No, Sasha, I don't want to die in America, I'd rather buy that Missoni swimsuit with the long ties and the golden buttons. He laughed, spitting a tiny piece of fried egg on my hand.

Sasha was the closest person to me, but it wasn't enough. A comforting diner breakfast wasn't enough, humor wasn't enough, what I needed he couldn't give me.

I walked him home to his dick tower then stopped at the

Whole Foods on Hanson for tomatoes. It had just opened, we had arrived in the neighborhood at the same time, it was a flag of gentrification and I opposed this of course, but I had to compromise. The tomatoes at the deli were flavorless, I tried the Stop & Shop near Barclays but couldn't make it to the produce section, the place smelled like a hospital. So I started going to Whole Foods, so what, only for the tomatoes. I am, after all, Mediterranean. I had to maintain some semblance of identity. I also bought thyme seeds there, to add to my collection of plants, all of them in the kitchen facing Fulton. Once a week, I dedicated a full hour or so to watering, trimming, repotting. It was the most I could do, as there was no nature for me to enjoy outside, only a locked park, uneven sidewalks, loud cars, even the people did not seem human.

I could never keep up with it. I think maybe that's what it was. That I couldn't keep up with my body. Or perhaps that my body couldn't keep up with me. That is always the question in my mind, but I don't know if you're any good at answering such questions. Did I do it to my body or did my body do it to me? Saying this aloud makes me realize that it is all rhetorical, that language is making me go about this the wrong way. We are not so different, my body and I. Often language is not enough, but in this case it's too much, it complicates.

L eonard interviewed his mother and the results were sensational. I sat on the trash can in my kitchen, reading his miniature blue handwriting and watching the sun rising through a slit between the skyscrapers.

Because I didn't have a TV in my apartment, and no one to talk to, I would read through the students' notebooks on Sunday mornings. I was tempted to buy a TV, they are very friendly and comforting. You can just be with them, passively, breathe and every few minutes swallow and once in a while go to the bathroom. But I couldn't do it, the TV advertisements freaked me out, they were always on opposite ends of the spectrum, on one end the fast food and cars, on the other end the insurance and pharmaceuticals. No, I couldn't buy a TV, I was scared of American culture. When I say that, I don't mean the right to bear arms, I mean wedding dresses and obesity.

For his composition, Leonard had interviewed his mother about her marriage. I read it enthralled, like it was a telenovela. I realized then that he was the most intelligent boy in his year, if not at Franklin, although he didn't speak much during class, he often kept his head down. His head was big and full of shiny black hair, in a bowl cut.

In response, I wrote him a long letter, which I stapled inside his notebook. I showered him with praise for his composition, which he truly deserved. He wrote clearly and concisely and, as far as I could tell, without errors.

I expressed sympathy for what he wrote had happened last Easter Sunday and proposed that he restructure the interview so that the climax was a reveal of how his father had beat his mother up. I told him it would make the interview more compelling, and that the reader would be left with something to think about. He had quoted his mother saying that forgiveness is God's command, and so I also advised him that in the academic world biblical references are looked down upon as idiotic. But I know that you're a smart boy, and an independent thinker, I wrote, and this habit will soon cease by itself.

After that, I read through the other students' notebooks. My neighbor started playing the clarinet in the background, while I corrected spelling mistakes and made small notes in the margins. The last notebook in the pile was Carl's. I want to die, he wrote, I don't want to do this anymore, I will kill myself with a gun. He had written in pencil, his letters flooding the faint blue lines. I want to die, I'm going to kill everybody at school. I got worried, briefly, and for some reason I looked out the window at Sasha's momentous tower, with its copper dome and giant clock. I read the time, half past nine in the morning, as if the clock were ticking for Carl. He was the only Asian student in my class, from Chinatown, and he got a lot of shit for it from the other boys.

I then turned another page in his notebook and saw that he had indeed completed the composition, he had interviewed himself, imagining that he was the world champion of online poker. At the bottom of the page was a list of items including the new Beats headphones, some computer games, and other gadgets I didn't recognize. I thought, This kid still has something to live for. I ripped out the threatening page and never told anyone about it, certainly not Aisha.

I knew that what I was doing with my students was unorthodox, and that it could land me in trouble with that lousy and ineffective system of education. But I was beginning to see results. I asked the students to stand up while reading their compositions in class, to hone their confidence, and Leonard at first kept staring at the carpet but slowly I noticed him looking up, raising his voice, facing the inevitable exposure that it is to be alive among others, especially in New York, where he couldn't afford to be introverted. I also noticed that Sal had started to rhyme in his writing, and I encouraged him to take it further. I even gave him an Exclusive Exemption, as I called it, and allowed him to use swear words. I took the small things as grand victories.

The next weekend, I woke up, I ate my breakfast, I emptied my bowels, I did my skin-care regimen, and, for the first time that season, I wore my Cucinelli cashmere sweater. I had slept nine restful hours and woke up determined to act, to get clean.

It was a cold morning, I walked to the CVS on DeKalb and picked up everything I was missing. By now, cleaning was a science complete with a taxonomy. I bought soaps, sponges, brushes, and wipes of all kinds. I swerved through the aisles, focused, I got the feeling of being the only woman in the world, like for a moment I had become one with the store. When I got to the cashier I counted all of my coins, including the pennies, and paid with exact change.

Outside, I gave the rest of the coins to a homeless man. I don't remember what he said, but they were freezing cold, and there were so many of them that he had to bring his palms together.

The bags were too heavy to carry so I dragged the blue shopping basket out of the store and back to my building, up the three flights of stairs, a gallon of Clorox threatening to fall out. By the time I got inside my apartment, my movements were no longer steady, they were frantic. I filled the bathtub and transplanted myself into the boiling water, the CVS basket by my side.

I spent the rest of the morning immersed. I did it all, very methodically. There was the problem of dirt, as well as the problem of hair. Both were undefeatable. There was hair on my legs, on my arms, my underarms, from my belly button to my sex, which until then I had only trimmed when I absolutely had to, when it began to itch or smell whenever I crossed or uncrossed my legs at work.

I alternated scrubbing and shaving. I scrubbed my legs, then shaved them. I scrubbed my arms, then shaved them. I scrubbed my genitals, then shaved them, then scrubbed again. All the dead skin and hair floated around me in the water, my pubic hair sticking to my shoulders and chest. Then I began to specialize. I removed the nail polish from my toes and dumped the red cotton buds in the water. I clipped my nails, then used a thin wooden stick to clean underneath them, fishing miniature balls of wool from the sides. I pushed back my cuticles and clipped them. I scrubbed my feet, for a long time, tapping the pumice stone to the bathtub floor so nothing remained in its pores. Then, when I judged my feet to be soft and clean enough, I scrubbed them with the Turkish hammam loofah. I climbed up from my feet, to my calves, to my thighs, to my labia, to my asshole, to my belly button, poking soaped fingers and makeshift tools wherever I could.

After cleaning, I paused. I paused to feel this new body, a transformed body. You and I pause too sometimes, but ours are the uneasy pauses of two strangers. With time, we are getting to know each other.

That day, I had created something. I called it the CVS Retreat, because it always started at the drugstore, and spending money was a prerequisite.

No, nothing changed, nothing helped. But I was doing something, I was working hard. I unstopped the plug and let the water drain out. While it drained, I washed my hair and soaped every slope of my head and body, keeping my eyes on the bathwater, on the emerging tundra underneath.

It was the most magnificent sight. A light-brown speckle, the color of my skin, which is also the color of dirt. Then thin long hairs like supple grass, clusters of pubic hair like spindly bushes. A film of slimy soap, the primordial matter pooling around the dead bodies, the red nail polish on cotton balls. Snakes and cuticles in rows like limestone terraces. It was beautiful like summer in Palestine, uneven and seared. I bent down and collected all of it in my palms, a dry wind pushed the bathroom door open.

walked out and stood in the center of the living room. The skylight brought in the sun, and at noon it projected a perfect square in front of the full-length mirror. I stood in its spotlight, the sun was bright, casting almost no shadow behind me. I looked at my complexion in the mirror, I was pale, all this scrubbing was brightening my skin.

I lay down at the center of the sunny square. The hardwood floor was warm, it relaxed the muscles in my back, and I felt my shoulders softening into the hard surface.

I took deep breaths, like I was at the beach. I look white, I thought. And I didn't like looking white, because I'm not, I'm Arab, with a deceiving complexion. I then briefly felt sorry for myself for being Arab, although luckily, as I said, it wasn't so obvious with me. I could look like anything, I blended in wherever I went.

My neighbor then started playing the clarinet again, and I turned over to tan my back. At first I just heard random notes, here and there, but slowly something came together. I lay there, in the warm sunshine, listening to my neighbor's music. It took me a few seconds to understand what was playing. It was nothing classical, of course, if it were I wouldn't have known it. It was "Bella ciao."

Now I'm going to tell you something, and I want you to be open-minded. I promised to be honest with you.

The clarinet moved something inside of me. It was nothing scary, just a gentle vibration with certain notes. It was in the center of my back, on my spine, in the place I could not get to, not with the Cattier Method nor with the Turkish hammam loofah. While the chorus of "Bella ciao" played over and over again, the movement became rhythmic. At first it just wobbled, heating, until it got much hotter than the rest of me, until finally it was blazing and spinning inside my body. And then I understood at once. It was the coin. I had no doubt about it, I just knew. I had put it there when I was little, in the car ride down south. For more than two decades the coin was gone, I didn't know where it was. And then, for some reason, in New York, it was resurrected.

It was a strange feeling but not unpleasant. I can even say that it was satisfying, because I came back the next weekend and did it again. By the time I finished tanning, the sunny square had shifted to a parallelogram, one of its sides climbing the wall and the mirror, and the coin slowed down to a halt. I turned around and gave my face just five hot minutes, hoping for a slight bronze on my cheeks and forehead. I stood up to look in the mirror. My neighbor finished practicing, and it had worked, I was darker.

From then on, my neighbor, the coin, and I did this every Sunday, starting at half past noon. Once I got properly dark I allowed myself a certain degree of freedom. Instead of timed intervals of belly to back, I curled into the fetal position inside the sunny square, flipping the coin, taking short, restless naps, sometimes singing along.

That evening, I stood Sasha up and went to Times Square. I was very clean and put together. I wore my Dolce & Gabbana coat, silk black pants, a full face of makeup with red lipstick, and my Dior hat with the pink ribbon. I had been increasing my intake of fluids, drinking more and more lemon water, grinding turmeric into my tea. My face was like honey and I liked what I saw in the mirror. When I smiled, that is. My resting face was terrible, that has always been the case, my childhood was too difficult. But when I smiled, really, I could see that I was healthy, that my teeth were white and my lips were plump and my eyebrows were thick and black and obedient.

When I first moved to New York, I used to look at people everywhere I went. I looked at them like they were living artifacts. I saw details, I imagined what their lives were like, I pushed to make eye contact. But very soon I stopped doing that, I lost interest. It was too crowded and they all started to look the same to me, they all wore that Uniqlo nylon jacket, they were all miserable, overworked, and joyless. I didn't care for them, and they didn't care for me.

It's a terrible thing, habit. That's another reason I always have to leave. I don't want to be complacent.

I got off at Forty-Second Street, and there, with the tourists, it was different. They were unaccustomed, they were fresh, like my boys, and immediately I saw myself in their eyes. They all looked at me. The Spanish girls looked at me, the Midwesterners with mascara on their lower lashes looked at me, even the Israelis looked at me. Women with tired feet raised their heads and looked at me, Norwegian couples with bags and bags of shopping looked at me, friends in groups of three and four and five, they all looked at me. They all looked at me and they all saw something.

I stood there for a while, at the intersection of Broadway, Seventh Avenue, and Forty-Second Street. I watched the people, the big screens, they soothed me. At one point, I thought I saw my student Sal entering the army-recruiting station, although it was not possible, he was too young.

I couldn't handle more than twenty minutes standing there in Times Square, my neck began to ache from looking up at the screens, but it was enough. I could see myself in their hungry eyes. I could see my mysterious and exotic beauty, it was not a lie, it was the truth.

It was also the truth that I was lonely, miserable, and tired. But it was a truth that I had begun to rearrange as one rearranges a closet in the transitional seasons.

had two groups of clothes: Darks, which accounted for 95 percent of my wardrobe, and Whites, of which there were only a few items. The Whites: undershirts, underwear, and socks. The rest of my clothes were all black, gray, or navy, which is the only color that can compete with black. Cotton oversize pants from Marni, faille pants from Chloé, two identical pairs of wide-leg raw denim from Gucci, wool pants from Miu Miu, silk pants from Bottega Veneta. The tops: two sleeveless tunics from Theory, a Simone Rocha cotton top with ruffles at the bottom, a Valentino T-shirt with structured lace sleeves, a mesh blouse from Fendi, a linen V-neck with a zipper on the side from Prada which was very tight and flattering, two basic long-sleeve shirts and two turtlenecks from Wang, a flaming-hot cashmere sweater from Brunello Cucinelli, a reclaimed cashmere sweater from Stella McCartney, and an Issey Miyake pleated ensemble. I also had a miniskirt from Celine and that dress from Alexander McQueen. The coats and jackets: one Max Mara blazer, one Dolce & Gabbana floor-length wool coat for December to February, one Burberry trench coat, although by then of course I had left it by the orange bin outside my building.

It wasn't much, but it was enough to look consistently chic and expensive. Don't forget that I came to New York with just one suitcase. I could have bought more clothes there, what else is there to do, but the fashion house of Vetements convinced me against it.

That fall, Vetements erected a massive pile of clothes in the center of Saks. The big pile was mostly jersey and denim, in all the colors I despised: faded black, army green, sports orange, fire-extinguisher red. It was a big pile of rags, like soccer-mom laundry, a monument for mass consumption.

I really admired this brand, even though I didn't own anything from there, it was the opposite of my taste. Those brilliant Georgian designers were like the Banksy of fashion, they sold sweatshop hoodies for thousands of dollars, because the young and ultrarich wanted to look like the working class. The slogan was Ugly Is Beautiful.

Of course, it's very cruel, but it's a reflection of the truth, isn't it, that the truth is ugly. I used to think that if people saw the real face of wickedness, not the mask, then they would revolt. I used to be a proponent of transparency. When Netanyahu and Trump were elected I thought those were good days, because the truth had come to light. But it seemed not only that the truth was ugly, but also that ugly was beautiful. The people adore the monster, the rich want to look poor.

On Monday, I prayed that Sal wouldn't show up at school. I prayed that he would be sick, or have a basketball tournament, or have to stay at home to take care of his younger sister. And of course, as soon as I turned the corner of First Avenue, I saw him standing outside the school entrance, chewing a big ball of green gum before eight in the morning.

Sal was a handsome and stylish boy, but a needy and problematic student. He was a family relative of Aisha's, and I suspected that she had gotten him admitted to Franklin under the table, because it was clear that he was academically inferior to the other boys and couldn't have fairly passed the entrance exams. He was moody, unable to control himself, at first he would whine, and then if I didn't pay attention to him he would get aggressive and start barking.

After lunch that day, he took a seat next to Jay. I announced to the classroom that we were going on a trip on the Wednesday before Thanksgiving, to a poetry reading in New Jersey, and that I was going to take them out for burgers afterward. The class erupted. Burgers, double, cheese, could they get bacon, fries, and sodas.

After a while, they calmed down, but Sal wouldn't, and he kept complaining that I had made him hungry. He started sharpening his pencil, over and over again, breaking the tip on the page, then blowing it on the floor. He also picked on Leonard, asking him repeatedly what he got on his math quiz and what he ate for lunch. I couldn't tolerate anyone distracting Leonard or Jay, and normally I would have confronted Sal, but that day, I couldn't. I told him to come sit next to me behind the teacher's desk. It was easier that way, because I didn't have to look at him.

The night before, Sal had showed up in my dream. We were sleeping in the kids' bedroom in my grandmother's house, a room that was raspberry red with two little beds. We kept tossing and turning at night, both of us, and at some point I heard him sighing in the dark. I walked over to his bed and got underneath the sheets.

In my dream, Sal was eighteen years old. It was a knowledge that I possessed in the dream, and I'm not saying this to cover up pedophilia. He looked the way I knew him, but older. He was already a good-looking young man, with a square head and hairline that reminded me of Muhammad Ali. In the dream his shoulders were broad, I lay on top of him, he hugged me, his skin was warm, and I felt his erection on my belly. We started to kiss and I breathed into his mouth and then I took off his basketball shorts and I was so wet that he penetrated me without effort. We had sex for just a second before I realized who he was, he was my student, Sal Ando. I jumped out of his bed and turned on the lights in the raspberry bedroom. In place of the closet was a big blackboard with scribbles in pink and yellow chalk. I began erasing them in a panic, so terrified of what I had done. I can't remember what was written, but I remember the letters C and A. Sal called to me in the dream, but I couldn't turn around, I couldn't look at him.

When the bell rang, he tapped my shoulder. Miss, he said, Miss. He was suddenly very polite, like he was grateful to have been invited to sit next to me during class. What? I asked. He reached his hand to my neck, I pulled away from him, but he had touched me. Nothing, he said, You had something there. He had picked something from my neck, and it landed on my desk. It was a hair, and I knew, without a doubt, that it was one of my pubic hairs.

There is a photograph of me, I am five years old in my grandmother's house, naked, carrying a broom.

My grandmother's house was immaculate. It had Prussian blue walls, Murano glass lamps, and a walnut record console that alternated the Arabic classics with American swing. After lunch, we would sit in the salon and she would tell me a story from her youth, either glamorous or tragic. She would then abruptly crush her Marlboro Red and go back to her day-to-day concerns, all revolving around the broom, the T-shaped mop, the bucket, the duster, the carpet beater, the garden hose, the metal-wire laundry lines sagging beneath the heavy white sheets.

My job was to sweep the garden, using a primitive straw broom. I swept the purple flowers of the jacaranda trees. I swept the stone steps, snaking through a terraced garden with citrus trees, pruned jasmine bushes, roses, and hibiscus. At the top of the steps was a lily pond with goldfish and koi, the flowers bobbing up and opening in the morning hours. I swept around it, pushing the dirt into the water. In the evening, before dinner, my grandmother would wash my broom while I sat in the swing underneath the grapevine.

But somewhere along my childhood, around the time of the

missing shekel and the car accident, the pond was emptied and filled with gravel and succulents. Then the grapevine was obliterated by a mysterious pest and the lemons got smaller and smaller each year, because no one was picking them anymore. A while later, in the twilight years of dementia, my grandmother hired a gardener from Jenin to cut down the jacarandas. She said that she couldn't keep up with them anymore. Having to sweep the flowers' carcasses every day was breaking her back.

Some days and nights, I just wasn't myself anymore. I had a hard time cooking, doing the dishes, vacuuming, getting on all fours to sort the recycling or check what was inside the bottom drawers of the fridge. I was easily irritated, I made mistakes. Even at work I was struggling. I stuttered in class, thinking more about my posture than what I was saying. I was too tired to stand, so I sat at my desk. I stopped going around the classroom to reassure the boys, one by one, because they were sweaty, and sometimes they smelled of semen. And also because I couldn't look them in the eye, there was a guilty look on my face, I wasn't always there.

Other days and nights, I was buzzing, I had so much energy that I could have jogged, or cared for a toddler. I could have cleaned not just my apartment, but every apartment in my building and on my block.

On one such night, I was preparing for bed, I turned off the lights in the kitchen, and I saw that there was a paper jam in my printer, blinking in the dark. I had bought this printer when I first moved to the apartment, I don't know why, maybe I thought a teacher needed a printer. It was a white HP model, erratic, I only used it a few times before it broke. I turned on the kitchen light and decided to put an end to it. I said to myself, I'm not a victim, a printer won't break my spirit, a coin is just an inanimate object. Yes, I was very sure of the coin by then. And I was attached to it, too, I could hold it in my thoughts. I was convinced that it was the cause of everything, that need for a tight grip on the universe, and especially the dirt. I was also afraid that maybe the coin had rusted, over the years, and was decomposing inside of me, or maybe it was multiplying, a small stack, three or four shekels, which, when I was a kid, was enough to buy a can of Coke.

It was midnight then, close to silence. It's a lie that New York never sleeps. I turned on the light and did it in a hurry, like someone was pushing me. I slid the printer onto the floor, flung it open, took out the ink cartridge, and when I saw the page I yanked it out so hard that the paper ripped, my elbow hit the bookcase, and my Lys perfume fell off the shelf and shattered on the living room floor.

I stood up and looked at the printer, still blinking, and it was also on the floor now, wide open, with the ink cartridge and broken glass. I considered putting the motherfucker out of its misery. I wanted to stomp on the dying animal and throw it out the window at the homeless man who slept at the bus stop. I was angry, no doubt, and at the same time, I was amused, happy even. It smelled of lilies. My horror turned unexpectedly into pleasure. I imagined myself going outside with a gun and spraying down Fort Greene with all its rich and poor. I could give the gun to one of the brothers who ran the Smoke Shop, tell him to empty it. He'd be glad to do it after I'd killed his entire family. Free Yemen.

When I went outside, there was a light drizzle and the trees were shedding their last yellow leaves. I put the bag of broken glass in the recycling, it dropped like a cymbal, and then I looked inside the bins and decided to sort their contents. I did this quickly, to stay warm. It was already November and I wasn't wearing a jacket, only my Miu Miu pants and a shirt from Wang.

When I flipped the orange bin on the sidewalk, one of the Yemenite brothers saw me as he was shuttering the Smoke Shop, but I said assalamu alaikum in an American accent and pretended like everything was normal. I only managed to sort one bin, the one intended for paper recycling. Maybe I had hoped to find my trench coat, but it had been nearly two months since I had abandoned it, and there was only garbage.

I found two plastic cups, one smelling of bad milk, one with a bit of iced tea. I poured the liquids out into the gutter and put the cups in the plastic recycling bin. I also found a pizza crust, a half bagel with egg and avocado with a napkin still stuck to it, two lollipops, a chamomile tea bag, an apple core, and a baby's pacifier with the chain still attached. Surprisingly, there was a bit of paper in the paper recycling bin, and boxes from Amazon, which

I flattened and arranged neatly inside. This only took me fifteen minutes, and all in all I had enjoyed myself.

When I finished, I went to the liquor store that was open late, bought four mini bottles of Chivas, and took small sips all the way to Sasha's building. Ta, ta ta, ta. He didn't open his apartment door, he was asleep, so I asked the doorman for the spare key, telling him it was an emergency. I did really look like I had just run out of my house to deliver some very important news.

I woke him up, I started to undress and I got on my knees, and of course he fucked me. I was filthy from the garbage outside, the trash had seeped into my skin with all the rain, I smelled like my perfume and I was burping Chivas. I licked his beard, it stank of me, I held onto his hairs with my teeth, I wanted to rip some out, but he flipped me over and told me to shut up and then he fucked me until I blacked out, not alcoholically, but in the sense that I had transcended the present.

I woke up in my bed at home and the pants from Miu Miu were outside the apartment door and the shirt was in the laundry. So I suppose I had done the right thing and gone home and got clean.

There is a logic to organizing. Everything has its place, even the tiniest scrap fits in a closed ecosystem. There is no excess, the mosquito is as essential as the chimney, the tea bag will be reborn an eagle. Even the shekel is a native of this earth, mined from the depths of Chile or Utah. Sorting brought me comfort, order is relief.

The next day, I found my trench coat. Not where I had left it by the orange bin, but on a man. I saw him from across the street, outside the Citibank on Lafayette, waiting, waiting for me, I suppose.

The light turned green, I began crossing the street, and I recognized the coat, the Burberry epaulets and belt loop. I walked quickly toward him, in a straight line, and as I got closer, I began to feel like there was actually no need to rush, that this was a secure transaction. I approached him quietly, and he turned around and looked at me, as if we knew each other.

His eyes were far apart, his hair slicked back, his skin was tan, dry, as worn as a shoe sole. He must have spent all of his childhood in the scorching sun. I like your coat, I said. Thank you, he answered, very courteously, it's Burberry. I know, I said.

I took a step back and examined him without shame. Underneath my coat he was wearing a navy pinstripe suit, slim-fitting, and brown leather boots. He was not much bigger than me, the coat fit him well, Burberry is made for tall girls. He extended his hand, it was covered in little scars and a silver Rolex. I was on my way to the bank in order to cash my brother's check, and my hand was still inside my Birkin, squeezing the envelope. I took it out and shook his hand. He grinned, a big smile. I kept staring at him, at the coat, at the belt with the stitching and D rings. Do you want it? he asked, then began taking it off. What? No, no. Why not? It's yours now, I said.

He waited for me while I was in the bank, and when I came out, we crossed the street together and he walked me back to my building. I saw that a green thread was holding one of the tortoiseshell buttons. It was definitely my coat. I had resewn the button after it got caught in a banker's umbrella, and I used a green thread on purpose, to mark my territory. Do you come to this neighborhood a lot? I asked. Almost never, he answered. He told me that he was an art dealer, that he was in my neighborhood to visit an artist. I showed him where I lived but he didn't say that it was there that he had found the trench coat. He only kept looking at me, making eye contact, the gentle kind that made my heartbeat slow down. He asked me if I'd like to meet the following day. I told him I had a very busy schedule, I was a teacher, but that I could meet him next weekend. He nodded in understanding and said he would pick me up next Friday, Black Friday, at nine in the morning.

As I entered my building, he stayed standing outside the glass door, waiting for me to climb up the stairs. In my apartment, I took out the cash from my Birkin and started accounting. It was something I had never done before, not with such diligence. I had started cashing my brother's checks at the branch on Lafayette and carefully following my spending, to the cent. At first, my wallet carried ten thousand five hundred and thirty-two dollars. And then, slowly, there was an inhalation and exhalation of the leather. A bill would be broken, I would have less but it would look like more. Then the accumulation of coins, less money but the wallet became bulkier. Then, after a CVS Retreat or a donation, the animal got light but never hungry. In my head,

I kept a seismograph of my consumption, my generosity, my oscillating worth.

Ever since the coin reappeared I started looking at money very differently. I had to pay the shekel back, or maybe I was already paying, in small painful installments the size of slow hours.

On Wednesday, on the train to New Jersey, the students started asking a lot of questions. How long is it going to take, where are we having burgers, is this technically a free class. I said that many people would be there, not just the poet, and there would be music too, but we would make a group decision and leave whenever we wanted to. They all exchanged looks, an agreement that they were wholly uninterested in the poet, that they just wanted the burgers.

It was a warm day, the boys had taken their jackets off, and I walked down the aisle of the train and put them all in the overhead shelf. When the train started moving, I taught them how to do an autonomous head count. They had each been assigned a number and they were to call their number out loud, a ranked count-off. Leonard, my top student, was number one. Jay, my helper, was number two, and so forth, until we got to number twenty, which was Sal. Maybe it's a military technique.

After that, the ticket conductor came and went and the boys made fun of him, the way his nerdy voice cracked when he shouted, Tickets out. It was mean but I didn't reprimand them. Because fuck it, we weren't at school.

The coin had changed my personality entirely. I was impatient, impulsive, harder to please. My threshold for everything was lower. But on that day, out of school, out of mind, with the apartment spotless, wearing my Issey Miyake ensemble, I felt happy and relaxed.

I sat next to Elijah, number eight, and Ahmed, number twelve. Elijah was wearing a red button-down shirt with his black jacket, and I noticed that his ankles were hanging outside of his dress shoes. Ahmed was bigger than the rest of the boys, surely bigger than me. He was at that stage when there was no accordance between the body and the interior world. His delicate round glasses were always covered with oily fingerprints, and he had the beginnings of pink acne around his mouth. Like many of the taller boys, he slouched, his book bag was too heavy.

Ahmed was showing Elijah his drawings, pencil on A4, not good at all, but I appreciated his artistic spirit, and when he showed them to me I told him that they were great and asked him if he had more. I even told him that there was a competition that he could enter, but to tell me in advance so I could help waive the five-dollar entrance fee. I wanted to encourage him to keep drawing, but I didn't want him to waste five dollars on a contest I was certain he was going to lose.

When we came out of the tunnel into the clear New Jersey sky, Ahmed asked me if I liked to draw. I told him I didn't, but that my brother was a famous graffiti artist in my country. This wasn't true, of course, although it was true that my brother was good at drawing. He had taken all the heritable talents, he was very artistic, he could draw anything, and he was also very musical and could pick up any of my father's instruments and play them without difficulty.

I told them that where I was from there was a big concrete wall, that we were living in a time of segregation, like in the American South not so many years ago, and like in South Africa, which they knew about from a recent lesson about the Soweto uprising. My brother was very well-known for his artwork on this wall, I told them. Then I pulled up a few Banksy images on my phone and showed it to them. Ahmed jumped up from his seat and wanted to show the other boys, so I gave him my phone. Don't press anything, I said.

When we got to Newark, I took them to the kiosk in the station. I asked the manager if my students could leave their book bags in the back and explained that we would return in a few hours. As a gesture of my appreciation, I let the guy's hand touch my ass when I squeezed out of the stockroom. I don't think any of my students noticed.

The air was clearer in New Jersey, a spring day in November. I had been tanning regularly, and nobody could have mistaken me for being white. The insides of my arms were light, like coffee with too much milk, but my forearms, shoulders, and hands were brown, and my knuckles, as well as my elbows, my knees, my scars, the inside of my belly button, and my labia, if anyone were to look, were even darker, a brown created from blue.

It was a few blocks before Jay's fingers relaxed in between mine, until he finally raised his head from the ground. We walked in a group, crossed the street together, toward the park downtown, following the sound of amplified voices, speeches, the words still too distant to make sense of, then song, then an applause like fire.

When the poet was introduced, I gathered all the students and we entered the crowd. If the FBI were to ask how many people had shown up downtown, then they would have found twenty more bodies than anticipated, young and naive for now but steeped in the whisper of war. I saw the boys looking at the crowd as they snaked through. Jay's hand was moist, and now that I think about it, he had every reason to be overwhelmed, because he didn't know where he was going that morning, and he was only fourteen.

The poet started to read and I squeezed to the edge of the stage, the boys behind me. The poet looked at the crowd when he read, especially at the boys. I knew that the students would imitate me, that this was a behavioral lesson, and when I put my fist up I saw that even Jay was clenching his, next to his thigh.

After the dagger poems, I called for a head count. Each student shouted his number, from one to eighteen, and then there was a silence. Number nineteen was missing, it was Carl.

I looked around for him, he should have been easy to spot in the crowd, but I couldn't see him. The boys saw me panicking, they started looking for him too, and they kept trying to split off. I said to them, Stick with me, boys, we're a unit now. But the only way to keep us together was to repeat the military count in a loop, with myself shouting the number nineteen.

We found Carl inside the kiosk at the train station, between the aisles, trying with all his might to get lost because he crouched near the floor when he heard us, pretending to examine a can of Folgers. I bent down to talk to him, so the other boys wouldn't see or hear us. What's the matter? I asked him. He pouted, said he wasn't Black, so what's the point. Well, Carl, are you white? I asked. He shook his head. Are your parents rich? He shook his head again. Are you happy? He looked down, and a tear fell on the vinyl floor of the kiosk. I'm not happy either, I told him. I then took his hand and we joined the rest of the boys outside. I said, Lose the ties, boys, we're going for burgers now. Some started swinging them over their heads in ecstasy, and others, Sal in particular, insisted on keeping them on.

In the line for burgers I tasked Jay with collecting the orders. They could get whatever they wanted, but no food was to be thrown away, so they must only ask for what they could finish. I gave Jay my card and told him to pay because I needed to sit down for a minute. He showed me the list to confirm. Ten double cheeseburgers with fries and Cokes, six bacon cheeseburgers with fries and Cokes, two double bacon cheeseburgers with fries and Sprites, one double bacon cheeseburger with fries and

onion rings and a Coke, probably Ahmed's, because he said he
had skipped breakfast that day, and, strangely, one Black Dada
Nihilismus burger with fries and a Coke. I told Jay, Very well but
my back is hurting, can you get me a veggie burger, fries, and a
bottle of water? The PIN is 1000, I trust you.

We ate quietly, awkwardly, for a moment I wasn't sure if they
were self-conscious about the dripping ketchup and mayo or if
they were just focused on not wasting my Mastercard burgers.
But many of them thanked me outside the joint, some wanted
a hug. I was feeling too much, no longer available. I suppose we
went back to the kiosk to pick up their schoolbags, although I can
no longer remember. On the train I slept.

When I was four, I discovered my skin color. Every summer, my grandmother would open the double doors for me, a big smile on her face, and shower me with praise. I was so beautiful, so clever. But why did I spend so much time in the sun, why was I so black? She would reprimand my mother for letting me look like that, they would have a short conversation, perhaps a fight, and my mother would leave and only come back weeks later. All of August I helped my grandmother with the cleaning and gardening.

We only went in the garden in the afternoons, in the shade. We picked the ripe fruits, before the birds got to them. We picked lemons, oranges, and grapefruits every day, before they fell to the ground. We weeded, relentlessly, and then we watered.

One day, we were in the lower level of the garden, near the pecan tree. My grandmother was deadheading the roses, and every time she touched a branch, it would spread the flowers' scent in the warm air. She told me to come closer, she was going to show me how to do it. She held on to the dried bloom with her left hand, counted down to the nearest set of leaves, and cut above it with a pair of old shears. When it was my turn, I held on to the dried bloom in my left hand, took the shears in my right hand, and my grandmother held my wrist, to show me where to cut. I looked at the back of my hand, the fingers, the thin wrist, against my grandmother's. I saw then that my skin was white. Up until then, I was convinced that I was black, or at least very dark. But in that moment, I saw the true tone of my skin. All things considered, I was light-skinned, the same color as my grandmother.

On Thanksgiving Day I performed the CVS Retreat, the Cattier Method, tanned in the sunny square, and sorted the garbage bin intended for plastics and glass. The next morning, Trenchcoat picked me up in a black Lincoln.

Trenchcoat occupied a different position in the city, I knew this when he suggested that we meet on a weekday. When you work, you belong to a certain class and its hours. You leave your apartment every day at the same time, get on the same train, stop at the same convenience store on the way home, always at the same time. I thought about that often, how there were millions of people in the city, like Trenchcoat, to whom I had no access, because we were living on different schedules. This also meant that I shared time and space with a finite group of people, and no matter how many times we came across one other, we would always be strangers.

Trenchcoat took me to Tavern on the Green in Central Park, where I sat on the pink velour armchair. When the waiter came with champagne, we both humiliated him by declining, No thank you. I'll have an Americano. Just bottled still for me. He ordered the French toast, said he had a sweet tooth, pointing at the missing molar at the edge of his smile. He complimented me on my teeth, Like pearls, he said, and told me he'd never been to a dentist. After eating, I went to the bathroom, the bathroom at Tavern was magnificent, I liked being in there. I thought it might be a good place to recompose myself if I was ever stranded uptown. I looked at myself in the mirror and smiled, and it was true that my teeth were pearlish, they were almost blue, which is the opposite of yellow. When I returned to our table I did not take the velour but sat close to Trenchcoat, on the expansive couch with the turquoise stripes. We had a view of the room, mellow music was playing in the background, and to our right, a big window with a view of Central Park, early on a Friday, watching the locals. I like that woman's scarf, I said. Fantastic, he agreed, there's nothing like emerald in winter. Yes, I continued, and green is the color of envy.

I knew that his trench coat was mine, but I never said it, I didn't want to upset him. I could feel that he didn't want to talk about himself. He asked me why I didn't live uptown, clearly I could afford it, if I lived in Fort Greene. I explained that I wanted to be close to my friend who lived there, in the tower that looks like a dick, that he was the only person I knew when I moved to the city. Now you know me, Trenchcoat said. He then excused himself to the bathroom, which I had earlier recommended to him, telling him to pay attention to the pink veins in the marble above the sink.

He came back wearing the trench coat, holding my Dolce & Gabbana for me while I slipped my arms inside. He smelled good, like he had just applied cologne but very tenderly. I had no problem paying for breakfast. It looked and felt like Trenchcoat was my husband, like our assets were shared.

Trenchcoat was my return to glamour. When I say *return*, I'm not talking about the past, I mean a feeling inside, a feeling that I was good enough, very good, better than others, the best. I don't think it's arrogant to think this, I think it's natural, a way of being that can guarantee one's survival in the era of wolves.

I never again saw the black Lincoln, but over the next week, Trenchcoat continued to show up outside my door, and we would take a taxi or train together to Franklin, and after work, we would go uptown, or to the West Village, it didn't matter where, as long as there was beauty there, like a good view of the city, or a linen napkin folded with great care, or a metallic pair of shoes that would make us both giddy.

It must have been about a week after our first date when he came to sleep in my apartment. That day, I was wearing one of my two pairs of Gucci jeans, the Fendi blouse, and the Celine brown leather boots. I remember it was a Saturday in peak fashion season, which is fall, because in fall you have a maximum range of options. You can wear a scarf, or a shaggy sweater, or almost any jacket, and you can also wear a skirt and flats. Unlike spring, fall is a great season for texture, for knit and tweed and velvet. And hats, of course. There is no better way to assert your confidence.

We had spent the day walking around, and we weren't big eaters but we had to eat eventually, so we had dinner at Cispedes, and again we both went to the bathroom, and again I picked up the bill.

In the evening, we got to my street, and it began to blow paper-thin leaves on us, like it was a snowstorm. I asked Trenchcoat to come upstairs. He twice said no, hesitated, then said yes. I felt my insides tighten like a rubber band. He was a man and I was a woman, the possibilities were endless. I became so excited, I dropped my keys. He picked them up, followed me up the three flights of stairs, and opened the door to my apartment. Just like I imagined it, he said, then he slipped my keys into his pocket.

He undressed, I brought him a towel, hung his clothes near the open window, facing Fulton. While he showered, I looked in his pockets, it's what women do. His phone was locked, his wallet had four dollars in it, there was no credit card or ID. I looked at the trench coat, then I put it on, but it felt different, looser. I looked at the button with the green thread and I don't know why, but I ripped it off and threw it out the window. It's my coat, I thought, I can do whatever I want with it.

That night, I skipped the Cattier Method, but I did everything else with diligence, I even got a small snake from my right arm, which by then was a rare accomplishment. I got underneath the sheets, naked, and Trenchcoat hugged me. His body was smooth, but it was cold, and there was nothing hard about it. I reached back to his thigh, to his groin, there was nothing. I took his hand and made him cup my breast. Then he said, Not like that. The rubber band inside me snapped. I pushed him away from me and turned to sleep on my stomach. He fell asleep quickly, but I didn't. I didn't understand why he didn't want to have sex with me, he was a man, I was a woman. I felt his masculine energy radiating underneath the covers, there was no question about it. So I stayed up, listening to his breath.

Do you know how rare it is to make a friend? You can't control it, it just happens to you, and when it does, it's enchanting.

We are friends now, aren't we? I wanted to tell you this story so I wouldn't forget, but now I also want us to be close. And I'm starting to enjoy myself.

In the morning, Trenchcoat was already dressed in his uniform, standing above the bed. I want to make you breakfast, he said. Good idea, I answered, my wallet is in my bag, there's a Whole Foods on Hanson. He was very quick. By the time I was finished with my morning ritual, breakfast was waiting on the table. Freshly squeezed orange juice, a thin butter omelet, toast, and croissant. We ate and left the apartment together. At Lafayette, I took a right to the subway station. Trenchcoat took a left and said he was going to the bank.

When we returned from Thanksgiving break, I saw my first parent at Franklin. It was Leonard's mother, she had a big silver cross around her neck. I said hello, introduced myself, and she didn't even smile. I continued up the stairs to my classroom, leaving the CVS basket at the entrance and carrying the student notebooks in my arms. In my classroom, I closed the door and looked through the eighth graders' notebooks. My fear was confirmed, Leonard's was missing, his mother must have read the manipulative interview and come here to complain. I went back down the stairs, through the administrative office, to the staff bathroom. I saw his mother sitting at Aisha's desk, and when I walked by the two became quiet and Aisha's head tilted, noting that I was going into the bathroom again.

That morning, I was supposed to teach the sixth graders a science fiction book, something from the old syllabus. Myself, I knew nothing about the genre, but it was all the boys ever wanted. They came in, all doe-eyed, but I couldn't stop thinking about Leonard's notebook and his battered mother. So I gave them a free class. I closed the door of the classroom, turned off the lights, told them it was nap time. On the door I stuck a yellow Post-it Note, Please do not disturb, and barricaded it with a broom.

During lunchtime, I looked for Leonard but couldn't find him. I asked Aisha if everything was all right. We were sitting around the tiny round table in the staff room, I was eating a salad Trenchcoat had prepared for me. Matthew was also there, the math teacher Sal always imitated because of the gay tone of his voice, and Gregory, the chemistry teacher. Aisha chuckled and said that Leonard's mother was only concerned that he didn't want to go to church anymore. Relieved, I wanted to go into the staff bathroom and put my feet on the sink again, but she started asking questions about our field trip. I tried to get it over with, I said that I thought it was important to take the students to New Jersey, so they felt connected to the periphery and not only to the center. Matthew choked on his falafel. All the boys are talking about how you had burgers at Shake Shack. Yes, I said, it was my treat. Silently, I thought, How can you think of burgers while eating falafel, you fat ass? And the poet, he asked, who was it again? Aisha didn't know him, neither did Matthew. But, of course, Gregory did. He asked if he was the 9/11 denier. No, definitely not a denier, but very vocal when Bush invaded Iraq. That was all I needed to say for the conversation to end. Nobody wanted to talk about anything that happened outside America, they only wanted to talk about food and television and the mold on the third floor at Franklin, which was giving everyone allergies.

After lunch, it was the eighth graders' class, and I finally saw Leonard. I began questioning him about the notebook, but he wasn't intimidated by me, he said he had taken it home with him, that he wanted to finish his New Jersey poem. I told him he wasn't allowed to take the notebook home, that if he wanted to write in it he could do so after class and I would stay until he finished. But why? Because I don't want you to have any homework. But all the other teachers give us homework. Well, I said, wouldn't you like it if the other teachers were like me?

I asked how things were at home. I did what Stokely did to his mother and asked how many people were living there. I asked him to name them and count them on his fingers, and eventually he also counted his father. I thought your father didn't live with you anymore, I said. He came back, he answered. And how has that been? It's okay, he doesn't yell at us anymore, Leonard said, he was born again.

After school, I asked Trenchcoat if he knew anything about being born again. I repeated the phrase a few times, but Trenchcoat had no idea what it meant, he had never heard of it, I think he was from a Catholic country. We crossed Houston, and I told him that my student Carl was from Chinatown, that his parents owned a plant shop on Worth Street. I'd like to see Carl's parents, I said, maybe I could talk to them.

Trenchcoat said he would lead me there, but he needed to make a business call. He walked ahead of me to Chinatown, I was irritated that he would abandon me for such a long call. It was noisy, I could not hear what he was saying or in what language he was speaking. I looked right and left for the shop, but mostly I kept looking at the trench coat. I almost missed it, on the other side of the street, Lucky Yu. I called to Trenchcoat, Go ahead, I'll meet you at the park where the old Asians play games. He covered the speaker with his hand when I spoke, like he was hiding me from someone, then made a quick gesture with his hand and walked away.

I looked through the store window and saw two women, maybe Carl's mother and aunt. I opened the door, a fake bell sound rang in the air, the women ignored me. I looked around the store, I said,

Hello, smiled, I wanted to make conversation but the older one was completely silent, and the other only said, Yes, hello, okay. I looked at the floor of the store, it was very dirty, not just with dry leaves and soil that should have been swept, but with stains and scuff marks that would require intensive scrubbing to remove. I looked at the plants, they were not in good shape. The palms were half brown, the vines were yellow and drooping, even the money trees were unpruned and unbraided. I tried to talk to them again, I pointed at a plant and asked what it needed, but there was no channel of communication.

Yu, the older woman yelled, calling for someone in the back. She was impatient, I think she was hoping I would leave, but I didn't. She then opened a door behind her, which led to a brightly lit staircase. Yu, she called again, but there was no answer. She glared at me and then yelled something in Chinese, adding the name Carl. I heard footsteps from above, and then Carl's voice, grunting, mumbling, getting closer. I silently waved with my arms, No, never mind, but he was coming down the stairs now, and I turned around and slipped out of the shop as fast as I could, the fake bell ringing behind me.

I put my head down, looped between the cars, crossed to a parallel street, walked in the wrong direction, and then turned toward Columbus Park. I caught up with Trenchcoat there. He was eating an ice cream cone in November, staring at the fountain, a brown paper napkin tucked into his collar like a bib. The sleeve of the coat framed the cuff of his white shirt, which was crisp and bright like meringue, although it should have been very dirty, living in the city.

Trenchcoat and I held hands on the walk back to Brooklyn. His grip was firm and as we got to the bridge, I told him, very matter of fact, I have a problem with my back, there is something stuck in there. He stopped abruptly in the middle of the bridge, an electric bicycle almost ran us over but swerved at the last second. Where, he asked, then touched the coin exactly. Yes, I said, how did you know? I know the human body, he answered, stand straight. I didn't want to, but I was already standing. You lean to the left, he said. What do you mean? I asked. He then held me by both shoulders and turned me around. He was strong, I rotated like a figurine in a music box. Your body temperature is uneven, that's why your left eyebrow is fuller. He ran his fingers through my hair and said, Hair is blood, hair is heat. It's not a big deal, he continued, then lifted his right knee up and pointed at it. We all have a weakness, mine is here, my brother stabbed me with a pencil when I was little, and lead is very pedantic.

We continued walking in silence. We were in the middle of the bridge now, facing Lady Liberty and Cuba. It was the perfect moment for a double suicide, but instead, Trenchcoat put his arm around my waist. When is your Christmas vacation? he asked. He didn't like my job, he thought it was beneath me, that a woman like me should not be confined to a schedule. December 16, I told him. Bella, he said, I just confirmed with them, on December 17 we'll be on a plane, we're going to Paris. I have work and you're coming with me.

He said that he could use my help with a job, that we would split the profits fifty-fifty, which I thought was funny because up until then I was paying for rent, food, transport, and cleaning supplies. I said yes, I needed a change of perspective. I told myself I would relinquish control. I knew that Trenchcoat wouldn't settle for anything less than five stars, his standards were even higher than mine.

When we got home I checked, but I could not see what Trenchcoat saw. I was beautiful, my body revealed no asymmetry. My eyebrows were identical, my breasts the same size, my arms the same length, my ears the same height. Even my myopia was symmetrical, negative one in both eyes. I turned my back to the mirror, shook my arms, my shoulders, and turned around at once, quickly, to see myself in the mirror. No, I do not slouch to the left.

After Trenchcoat fell asleep, I went through old photos on my phone, hoping that one would reveal something. I looked through the album of my uncle's second marriage. I am wearing a pink strapless dress, but in all of the photos I am holding a wine glass, or dancing with my arms over my head, or in one photo, I am standing next to my brother, indexing cake frosting from a long silver sword. It was a lavish wedding, and I always suspected that they used my money to pay for it.

When I was twelve, my uncle took me to the bank in Switzerland, to take care of administrative matters pertaining to my inheritance. We took the train in Zurich, it was my first time on a train but I had seen many of them in movies, and I knew exactly what to do, I took a seat by the window.

There were not a lot of people inside the train, it was spacious. I was wearing a matching set of gloves, hat, and scarf, in a bold pattern of electric green, yellow, and pink. I remember Zurich as very gray, grayer than anything I had ever seen before. It was like being a technicolor character in a black-and-white film.

My uncle handed me a bag of potato chips, paprika with a picture of sunflowers. The train began to move, it was quiet, nobody talked, I watched the streets rolling outside like a silent film. The train stopped at some stations, the people changed, blond people wearing coats and hats, like in movies about the Holocaust.

I took off my gloves and my uncle took them from me, so I wouldn't lose them. The bag of chips rustled as I opened it, and a woman turned around to look at me. I did not understand why, and I continued eating, then more and more people stared at me. I looked up at my uncle, at his mustache, and I was overcome by shame. I closed the bag and asked him for my gloves.

We got off at some station, I finished the bag of chips in the street and we couldn't find a trash can, so my uncle put the empty bag in his coat pocket, and it kept rustling as we walked through the bank.

My uncle was trying to take control of my father's inheritance, but it was impossible, my father was a scientist, he had thought of everything. My uncle showed me the safe and told me the password, which was *America*. I told you already, in my family, America was both the key and the curse.

A few days after Trenchcoat told me that we were going to Paris, I went to see Sasha. I wore his favorite dress again, the McQueen, and when he opened the door for me, there was already a bottle of white wine waiting on the kitchen counter. He poured me a glass, and I walked into the living room, in front of me the door to the balcony, or the suicide terrace, as I called it, with Lady Liberty and Cuba in the distance again. The sun was setting early, the sky was black and orange.

Sasha had a very strong instinct when it came to me. He read my moods, he even thought he could read my thoughts, and I knew it was just a matter of time before he found out about Trenchcoat. I put the glass down and lay on the couch, as if I were undergoing analysis. He sat on the armchair beside me, and we talked like this for a while. I told him that I had met a man and that I liked him very much. I continued, I described him, Sasha remained stoic, as if the matter was of no personal importance to him. I couldn't recognize a change in his voice, only that he was refilling his glass again and again, but I knew, from his questions, that he was assessing the threat. He asked what Trenchcoat did for a living, how tall he was, then chuckled. I raised my body from the couch, took a first sip of the wine. I felt that Sasha had dismissed Trenchcoat on account of his lesser masculinity, and I said, a bit angrily, Fun is very important, Sasha, don't underestimate the power of pleasure.

I stood up, slid the heavy glass door of the balcony, and stepped outside. The sun had set over Red Hook, the view less intimidating in the dark. We were twenty-four floors in the air, and Brooklyn looked like a children's game of blocks. I looked up at the clock tower, the minutes moving by, it was almost eight. I only ever looked at this clock between six and ten, I never saw the small hand pointing upward, or to the right.

I got close to the ledge and watched the city from above, the brick squares, the moving cars and yellow lines on asphalt. Sasha followed behind me. Don't you want to own a piece of America? I asked. Don't you want to own a piece of the earth? Owning an apartment is delusional, I explained, it's like breathing holy air, or drinking Zamzam water. It's like being buried in a vertical cemetery. After I said that, Sasha looked straight down, there was a police car parked on Hanson, across from the Whole Foods and the Apple store. It was always there. Look around, he answered, I'm the American dream, what more do you expect of life?

At my request, Sasha had applied Kinesio Tape to my spine, two strips, from the nape of the neck down to my lower back. The tape felt good, it didn't resolve anything but I felt that at least it held something in place, the coin was secure, I was no longer afraid of waking up one morning to discover that my spine had deconstructed and my torso was a bag of loose organs in the sack of my skin.

The tape stayed on for three nights before I woke up one morning and felt that it was now too dirty, it had to come off, there was no question about it. I could have peeled it myself, or asked Trenchcoat to do it, but I wanted something else, something more. I paced back and forth in my apartment. And then I saw my neighbor, from my bedroom window, a white woman playing the clarinet. Yes, a woman.

Are you interested in women? You must be, if you're here with me. I'm attractive in that convoluted way that women are attractive. But myself, I had hoped that the clarinet player would be a man.

She had short curly hair and the baggy body of an older woman. She held the clarinet so effortlessly, I envied her posture, the control she exhibited over her body, so much so that she could move her lungs while holding this object and make it sing. I knew the interior of her apartment well, I had often looked into it while lying in bed, studying the cushions on the couch, the microwave, sometimes the television when it was on. But this was the first time that I had seen her, the first time that I had seen the clarinet.

I knocked firmly. There was no response. Then I knocked in rhythm, ta ta-ta-ta ta, and I heard her voice, frightened, Who is it. I'm your neighbor, I said. She opened the door, she was taller than I had perceived through the window, and she looked at me distrustfully, up and down, but I had applied a thin layer of makeup before I headed over, and I gave her my best performance of harmlessness.

She invited me in, she was wearing an old pair of Levi's 501s. She asked me if there was something in particular that I wanted to discuss. I said yes, I improvised. There are some people always hanging outside our building and they are throwing their garbage in the wrong bins, I keep finding cardboard in the biowaste, chicken bones in the plastic. I would like to petition to the building management to put our bins behind bars, with locks. It's tedious, I said, but our planet is in decay.

Her name was Sofia, she gave me her email address. She said that she needed to continue practicing before her husband returned home. I instinctively scanned her apartment for photographs, I wanted to see the husband. Could I fuck him? I told her that I was a teacher, that I taught in a middle school in Manhattan. I looked at the kitchen, which was very similar to mine, with the same appliances, then back at her, and she looked at her kitchen and back at me and I realized that she wasn't going to offer me a drink. Which meant, of course, she wasn't going to peel off Sasha's tape.

I went back to my apartment and peeled it off myself. I stood still, a beat, nothing fell apart. There was no coin at my feet, no snakeskin on the sticky side of the tape. I put my shirt back on and went back to her apartment, the tape in hand, and I wrapped it around her doorknob. Touch it, bitch. It's yours now.

knew that this curse of mine was contagious, which was why I tried not to speak about it. I knew that I had infected one student at least, Jay, he wanted to stay with me longer after school, he became very attached to the cleaning. One day he told me, Miss, I have an idea, can you help me get on the table and the chair so I can Windex the clock? I had thought about it too, but I said, No need, it's clean, this classroom is the cleanest in Franklin.

I saw it in Trenchcoat too, he had picked up a few of my mannerisms, he had started drinking alcohol, for example, and I noticed that he was taking longer and longer in the shower and that my snail cream was depleting at an accelerated pace. One time, I saw him reach his arm behind his neck to scratch his back. It was a Cattier motion, and I saw him struggle with it and I knew that I had inspired it, that I had caused the itch.

Do you think I gave it to you or that you gave it to me? It's clear now that we both had it, but I wonder who had it first. Again, language is making me go about this the wrong way. Maybe it was like love, maybe we just sparked.

When I was with Trenchcoat I felt like a million dollars, and he became both my kingmaker and my valet. He walked me to school, carrying my CVS basket, and on rainy days he did so while holding an umbrella over my head. On the sidewalk, he always took the side closer to traffic, he was a man after all, and his job was to protect me. I took the side closer to the street people, I was better at dealing with them. If they got too close to him, his movements became unpredictable. Why are you standing in my way, he might ask, his tone polite but his face torqued in hatred. What are you doing on the ground, What are you looking at. In the subway, people watched us with a mixture of curiosity and contempt. If he liked a person, then he would smile and they would immediately approach us, and sometimes they would show up again, days later, and join us on our walk to school. If he didn't like someone, he was cruel, and he made them feel small.

One evening, we were sitting at Café Select, which was one of few places in Manhattan with a terrace on the sidewalk, a place to see and be seen. The cold was still mild, it was our last chance to sit outside. I was drinking profusely, to stay warm, and Trenchcoat was clutching a long cigar between his fingers, the paper emblem still attached. He didn't light it, he just moved it around, into his mouth, into his left hand, into his jacket pocket then out again. As if he was waiting for the right moment to circumcise it with his teeth.

I downed my third cognac and grabbed the cigar from Trench-coat, surprised by how it felt between my fingers. My uncle had smoked a lot, and I knew what a cigar should feel like. It should feel like a living thing in your hand, supple, aromatic, moist with saliva. But Trenchcoat's was dry, and too light. It reminded me of a plastic princess wand I had when I was a child. I used to wave it around the house, willing my desires.

I gave it back to him and asked the waiter for matches. Aren't you going to smoke it? I asked, it's dying. He thanked the waiter for the matches and placed them on the table. Well, he finally admitted, I'm not rich, you know. For now I'm just pretending. When I can afford it, I will start to burn them. He adjusted the Montecristo paper emblem, so it faced the street. I asked him, not for the first time, where he was from, and again he only answered that he was born in New York City.

Technically, Trenchcoat was homeless. It was not exactly a choice, he was dealt a bad hand, and the game is rigged, of course, it favors the better hand and exploits the weak. But at least in appearance, Trenchcoat was wealthy. He wore a perfectly tailored suit everywhere he went, he hung around the expensive neighborhoods, he smiled courteously at old women, he spoke slowly, enunciating all of the letters. His body was lean and strong, his posture the marker of good health.

Trenchcoat believed that one only belongs to a certain class inasmuch as one dresses, speaks, walks, shops, or takes as a certain class does. But his performance was not total. He smiled a lot, he felt comfortable in his own skin, something that made me suspicious from the beginning. Why is it that the rich are uptight and the poor are themselves?

renchcoat moved in with me, and he agreed to carry out certain duties.

Laundry is a refined art, one that requires great knowledge and precision, I said to him. And I don't have many clothes, so I always have to be washing. He agreed, he said he was the same. We were standing near the washing machine when we made the pact, the afternoon sunlight was shining through the window and onto his face.

The machine was not great, but at least it was my own. I couldn't share a washing machine with strangers, I couldn't tolerate their cat hair on my clothes, any hair for that matter, nor the lint of foreign colors. This machine was nothing like my old Bosch, and it confirmed my theory about Americans being dirty, in addition to being messy. The machine was called a top load, and it looked like a toilet bowl. When it turned, the clothes didn't really bump and grind, they just sank to the bottom and stuck to the edges. I had to soak my underwear in soapy water before washing it in this machine, and I didn't soil my underwear any more than other women do.

No, I don't think so, although I've never been tasked with cleaning the underwear of other women.

Every Thursday, I explained to Trenchcoat, I begin with the

underwear, socks, and undershirts, which I wash separately from everything else, because they need to be cleaned the most thoroughly. I stop the bathroom sink and fill it with warm water and two squeezes of Genie delicate detergent, stirring with a wooden spoon that I keep here. I opened the cabinet above the sink, another American thing that I found disgusting because I associated it with those orange pill bottles and the psychopharmaceutical complex, and showed him the wooden spoon.

Then, while it soaks, I wash the shirts and pants, only what can be washed by machine, of course. I wash these in one cup of gentle washing detergent, never with softener, on a delicate cycle, which only takes forty minutes. I opened the cupboard, showed him where I kept the detergents. When these are done, I continued, I hang them on a drying rack in the bedroom. It's in the closet, I'll show you in a bit. I never use the dryer, it's an enemy of clothes, and therefore an enemy of the earth. I also don't know how to use it, because I grew up in a hot climate, where a shirt dries during breakfast in the sun. You know what I mean, don't you? Of course, he nodded.

Next, I wash the underclothes that were soaking in the sink, also on a delicate cycle, with a half cup of detergent. Then I wash the towels, which are all white, two big ones, two small ones, and two washcloths. I use a cup and a half, and every other week I also add a spoonful of bleach, here.

We walked into my bedroom, I showed him the drying rack. There has to be a very clear partition in the rack, I explained. You have to balance it so it doesn't tip and collapse. Then, finally, I wash the bedsheets, also white. A fitted sheet, a flat sheet, one duvet cover, four pillowcases, 600 count. One and a half cup of each, hot cycle, bleach once a month.

I hang the pillowcases first, and then I drag that small radiator underneath the fabrics, on low heat. It looks dangerous because sometimes water drips on it, but believe me it's safe. Then I place the flat sheet on top of the drying rack, longways, then the duvet cover, patting it so it dries without wrinkles, and then, finally, I wrap the whole thing in the fitted sheet and spray a mix of eucalyptus and lavender all around. I close the room and all the windows and do what I need to do for the day. The laundry is like a cake that bakes.

No problem, Trenchcoat said, I can also do the ironing. We walked back to the washing machine, I watched him do it, and I made small corrections as he went along. Before he placed the sheets in the machine, he reached his hand inside and pulled out a coin, a quarter.

He didn't think much of it, but I took it as a bad sign. Ever since the coin had reappeared in my body, I had become very aware of the presence of money. I was especially concerned by how many coins there were out there and, at least hypothetically, all the damage they could do.

Is it really true that the poor are good and the rich are evil?

The boys at Franklin had never experienced a war, all the ones their country had waged were fought on foreign soil. I sometimes questioned my decision to go to America. I felt that I could have gone to Iraq or Yemen or somewhere in Africa, where the need for teachers is more dire.

You're right, I didn't have to go as far as Africa. I didn't have to go anywhere at all. I could have stayed home in Palestine.

But the answer is the same. I didn't have the courage to go somewhere dire. I wanted a certain life for myself. I wanted to give and to be good, but I also had a certain idea of myself, what my life should look like. Wearing heels was important to me. I couldn't have worn heels teaching in a school with dirt floors. The carpet at Franklin was bad enough as it was, the soles of my Louboutins were sometimes bluish. I haven't told you about all of my shoes yet, maybe I will get to it later.

It was Aisha who introduced me to Curls, they were together in some action committee. She excitedly told me about her Palestinian friend who was also in education. I emailed Curls, and we agreed that she would come to my class the following Tuesday with a guest, Rawda, who was a Syrian refugee and so presumably had a story to tell.

When they arrived, Rawda surprised me, so I suppose I had my own prejudices. I expected to meet an old hag in a headscarf and jilbab, but Rawda was about my age, with a bob cut that she had styled with a curling iron, wearing a black tracksuit. I later found out that she was actually Palestinian, a double refugee. It turned out that her grandfather and mine were both from Bisan. I didn't try to find anything in common, we were the third generation, it was too late.

Curls, on the other hand, was a classic Palestinian American, curly hair, big bust, big nose, and everything else petite but loud. The three of us had a coffee in the staff room, it was crowded so we all squeezed on the same couch. My boys are very smart, I told them, go ahead and talk to them like they are adults, they know a lot already, sometimes I read them the news.

I felt something warm around us, and I didn't know if it was blood, some visceral ancestral affinity. I was aware of our reproductive systems. I touched my elbow to Curls's left thigh, her hips were wide and fluid, they filled my mouth with saliva. Palestinians were losing on all fronts and I thought maybe a demographic offense was our only hope. I told the girls, If only we could raise children who were so committed that they were suicidal. I laughed, but they didn't have the same sense of humor, maybe it was a diaspora thing.

Rawda had an Arabic accent, but she kept saying, So, Like, As such. She had crossed over to Europe by sea from Turkey, four nights and three days on a plastic boat. It was this that the boys were most interested in, the boat, the sea, the storm on the second night, the burner phone she was given to complete the deal with the trafficker. They asked her about the toilets, of which there were none. What she ate and what she drank, which was water, fruit, and juice. This detail really enthralled Sal for some reason, he asked what flavor juice, and when she answered,

Mango, he shouted, Damn, I knew it. Leonard asked about the war, he wanted to know who was fighting who, and Rawda explained but it went over their heads. I didn't stop her even though I could see the boys were confused and losing interest. She talked about Assad's assault on Yarmouk and I was straining to put it all together in my own head. For a moment I felt like it clicked but then Sal cut her off and all the pieces drifted apart like continents. He asked her what she did with the juice box when it was done, if she threw it into the waves, what they did with the garbage in general as a boat must stay light and garbage is heavy.

I thanked Rawda and made the students applaud, then gave them their assignment. They were to write a story imagining that they were on a boat, leaving their country, not knowing if they would ever return or even make it to shore. They asked which country they were leaving. I said, The details don't matter, I want you to focus on the feeling.

Curls was standing in the back of the classroom, leaning on the wall. She smiled at me while I spoke, she crossed her arms, folded one leg on the wall behind her, which was already covered in blue shoe prints. It was the quality of attention she gave me. I noticed it, and I looked at her thighs again, and I wasn't shy because I felt that I was invited.

It was hard for me to say goodbye to Curls and Rawda at the end of class. I didn't have any girlfriends, and I would have liked them to stay longer. I wondered if they were going to get lunch together, what they did in the evenings, if they slept on soft or hard mattresses and whether there were traits that the three of us shared, like skipping dinner, or hugging a pillow between our legs while sleeping, or counting while brushing our teeth, or never getting into bed before showering. Now that I'm telling you this, I think what I wanted to know was if I was who I was just because, or if it had been programmed into me.

By the time we know ourselves, we are already. That is the problem of childhood. It takes you a couple of years to grow up, to be conscious, to make decisions, and by then it's already too late, it's just a race against those fateful years.

I'm going to tell you something else now, because I feel that we're comfortable. Yes, I'm talking to you. I wanted to know if you were a figment of my imagination or something inherited.

The next day, Sal was the first to read his assignment aloud. He cleared his throat in his usual exaggerated manner, he had the qualities of a great performer and could pace himself while reading. That day I even gave him permission to stand on the chair. Dear God, he began, looking at his audience. Oh Lord, he raised his voice, looking up at the popcorn ceiling, suppressing a smile, why have you abandoned me? I giggled, and I was glad Rawda and Curls were not there to hear this, although it was a legitimate question, even kids know that God abandons people every day.

Leonard's piece was dark, he mused on a beheading he had witnessed in the capital before boarding the last ship to Antarctica, a dissident, he used that word, who had spoken against the king and was dragged bleeding through the city streets. Did you read that in a book or see it in a movie? I asked. No, he answered, sitting back down in his chair, it was my idea, I like coming up with stories. Very well, your imagination is superb, Lenny. Can I call you Lenny? He smiled nervously, inhaling from his nose. Lenny, I want you to write the story of the dissident, a short story of two pages. I want to know what he did to the king and why he did it. Leonard smiled and proudly closed his notebook. Later, while another student read their assignment, I saw him open it again and write something down, a new idea.

Jay didn't want to read his story. That day, he sat in a corner in the back, like he was punishing himself. Later, at home, I checked his notebook and saw that he had written me a note. He wrote that he was feeling very sad, he couldn't do the homework. Then, War is bad, it kills people. I'm sorry Miss, I hope you won't give me an F.

I was worried for Jay. He was too sensitive, he had no shield. He was growing up in a culture that was over-legitimizing certain emotions, especially hurt, and encouraging vulnerability without discernment. Carl was depressed and empty, and he wanted to kill himself and everybody around him. Jay did not deny or deflect his suffering, he let it happen to him. Aisha encouraged the boys to talk about their feelings, there was always one boy or another sitting in her office looking melancholic, and later she would come to me and tell me to be easy on them, They're just kids. I told her that she was enabling depression and fostering mental illness. The brain is very malleable at that age, I explained. If you let them enter the dark alleys, they will remember the way forever, they will keep wandering back there as adults.

So I gave Jay an F on the assignment. I wanted him to be strong, to overcome himself. Take me, for example. I was still crossing the Brooklyn Bridge every day. And I didn't complain, because what good would that do?

Well, at the time I thought speaking would only make everything worse. But with you I see that naming the thing makes it smaller. Pain can be a great field of suffering, or pain can be just an object.

I did see Curls again. I emailed her to ask if she would like to get dinner, just us. I took her to Tavern, it was dark out and I couldn't see anyone in the park, so we gossiped about the other people at the restaurant, as if we were old friends spending meaningless time together. I paid, then asked her if I could come over, or if she would like me to rent us a room. We went to her apartment on the Upper West Side and when she got undressed I did everything to her that I would like a man to do to me. It was easy, familiar. I understood the noises she made and I answered like an echo. I had the feeling that I was doing it with myself, that we were doing it in a house of mirrors. Her kisses were soft, her skin smooth. At the end, I got a bit rough with her, because I'm used to men being rough with me.

We kept the lights on, and her studio wasn't bad either. The place was clean. I liked her bedsheets, they were a chalky pink and ironed. She owned too many things though, small things that cost less than twenty dollars. Those Armenian ceramic mugs from the Old City, copies of *The New Yorker*, candles, lint rollers, bottles of lotion, and vitamins. She was from Texas after all. But it was like masturbation without the void that feels like waking up from a nap and seeing that it's dark outside.

After we finished, things took a turn for the worse. She told me about her father's first marriage and her stepsister. She began to take form and character, dividing herself from me. The more she talked, the less I liked her. She wasn't bad, no, she was a pleasant woman. But the more she talked, the more separate from me she became, like she was stepping out of the mirror, her face distorting into someone else's, her curls tighter and her boobs more menacing.

With every joke she made I grew more and more distant, realizing that I was in the company of someone other than myself. Her Arabic too, it freaked me out. Texan Arabic, with that American impairment of the tongue and throat. It was impossible to speak with her in our mother tongue. We had sex again, but it wasn't the same. It was more complex, a dance, acting and reacting. It was too complicated, and I had to put an end to it and go back home to my Trenchcoat.

No, she wasn't hurt. Rejection is easier when it comes from a woman. It's like when I told Aisha that I couldn't come to the Brooklyn Museum because it was Sasha's birthday. She took it in stride, she even recommended a restaurant to me. Sex with women, I felt, was purely recreational.

The week before we flew to Paris, the weather changed dramatically.

By then, Trenchcoat was sleeping in my apartment every night, even when I wasn't there. I had come home one evening, not long after we made the laundry pact, and another one of his Italian suits was hanging in the closet, attached to a Berluti dust bag with some black socks and underwear inside. That was it. He had no other belongings, and maybe that's another reason the transition was so smooth, because his presence was light, not only in person but physically as well, he didn't take up a lot of space, he wasn't in bed when I woke up in the morning, he didn't leave any items lying around, no letters, no shoes, no bags or keys or change.

One morning, it was a Saturday, a bright day with near-freezing temperatures, and Trenchcoat and I had coffee at The Academy and then took the train to Fifty-Ninth Street. We went into a few stores on Madison, Trenchcoat opened the door for me even before the doormen could do it. I walked around the racks, touching the fabrics, while he mostly just stood there, observing from a distance.

At Prada, where they had just definitively changed to the triangle logo, I showed him a taffeta blouse. It was a great year for them and I wanted to buy it, but Trenchcoat convinced me that it was not practical, the sleeves were too puffy, I wouldn't be able to wear anything over it. At Hermès, Trenchcoat insisted that I get a new wallet, and I picked the red one in crocodile skin. At Loro Piana, the cashmeres were smooth, they felt like silk, and the suedes too, textureless to the eye and to the touch, like the skin of a young animal or a Russian woman. Trenchcoat picked a quilted gilet, the color of tea leaves, and told me he'd been very cold lately and needed to warm himself up. He also picked a white fringed scarf and draped it underneath my coat. Your clothes are very dark, he told me, you shouldn't wear a white collar, because you're a woman, but wear this scarf. I looked at myself in the mirror, and he was right, I looked better. I was now a picture in relief and not just a dark plane. How did you think of that? I asked, carrying the gilet and scarf to the cashier, paying for them myself, of course. Getting dressed, Trenchcoat told me, it's a cosa mentale.

We hadn't had any breakfast, and, like most people in the city, Trenchcoat and I ate just one meal a day. We went for lunch at The Mark, where Trenchcoat made friends with the waiter, his name was Dominic. I looked hard at Dominic and tried to read him. What kind of apartment did he go home to? Was it in the Bronx? In Astoria? Far away in Westchester County? Did he have a girlfriend or boyfriend, a mother, who relies on his paycheck? Or was he a spoiled kid, a wannabe actor or model, wishing to make it big in the city by rubbing against the rich and famous? Well, it didn't come up. In that servant uniform, with only a first name, Dominic was illegible to me.

Trenchcoat and I shared an arugula salad, chilled artichokes, pizza, pasta, and pinot noir by the glass. The price was high, but I didn't care. The value of money was not fixed, it fluctuated with my mood, with the weather, with the location. When the bill came, I took out all the cash and coins from my wallet, there was a lot of it, and it spilled out onto the tablecloth. Here, Trenchcoat said, then gently collected all of the money. Is it too heavy for you? I can take care of it, he said, then put all of my money into his pocket, turned away from me, signaled that we were ready, and when Dominic came, he took out the cash and paid without trouble.

When we left the restaurant of the hotel, Trenchcoat stopped by reception and told me to wait for him by the sofas. Guests were checking in and out, they all seemed to be in a hurry. I recognized their impatience, I belonged to that same demographic, except that it was a weekend, and now that I was with Trenchcoat, with a man, that is, I didn't have to worry about things getting done. Tables would be set, taxis would be called. With the right kind of man, I could be relieved of some burdens. I sat down, I thought maybe he wanted to get us a room, because we had had a wonderful day, and maybe it was time for us to have sex.

Trenchcoat approached the receptionist and I watched him from afar, his hands moving, not in unison but independently of each other, like he was conducting the conversation. He put a hand on his head, briefly, then again, then covered his ears. From the response of the receptionist, how she listened to him, I gathered that he wasn't reserving a room.

Yes, I was disappointed. Because I'm sure Trenchcoat and I could have had a lot of fun together. But many women would argue that a husband without the sex is an even better deal.

Dominic then appeared in the lobby and joined Trenchcoat and the receptionist. For a moment, Trenchcoat looked back in my direction but not at me. I noted that he possessed none of the traditional markers of male beauty, he was not tall, not broad, he did not have a strong jawline. What he had was a tension in his body, his chest open, his poise from another era, like he had never sat at a computer, never looked down at a phone or slouched on a couch. For me, Trenchcoat was a vision, a gentleman prince.

I stood up to join them, I wanted to know what they were talking about. Dominic said hello, Trenchcoat asked me if his hat was in my handbag, and of course it wasn't, because Trenchcoat had not been wearing a hat. Dominic asked the receptionist if anyone had seen a hat by any chance, that Trenchcoat had left it at the restaurant, or perhaps in the bar. The woman disappeared into a back room, then came back with a wooden box of lost and found items. Before she could even put it down on the counter, Trenchcoat said, There it is, reached his hand inside, and picked out a gray cashmere beanie. The concierge smiled in satisfaction, Dominic gave Trenchcoat a pat on the back. We exited the hotel and turned the corner. Trenchcoat looked at the label, said it was Barena, and put the hat on. It was the Trenchcoat way.

That evening, the TV was on in Sofia's apartment but I couldn't see her. I had a very primal craving for television, I reacted immediately to its hypnotism, like an animal instinct. Trenchcoat was out, and I lay there in bed, under the covers, and watched the images on the screen through the window. I would have liked to have had a radio as well, playing in the background, or the call to prayer. Not music, though, I couldn't listen to it anymore, I felt that it entered me immediately, dictated my emotions. Maybe that was why Sofia had such a strong effect on me. She was hypnotizing me with her clarinet, she was playing me, playing the coin, you could say.

At some point, I got a phone call from Curls. I was afraid that she was angry with me or, worse, that she missed me, but she only wanted to invite me to an event that she was organizing. A fundraising gala in February, in honor of our country. Those were her words, not mine, whatever they meant, because we didn't have a country. She said it was an opportunity for me to meet some comrades in New York. Her words again. It's not that I didn't care, I cared very much. But I was my own person, original. I had chosen to stand on my own two feet and walk out of that crooked land. I told her, I bet all the girls will be wearing traditional embroidered dresses, those don't look good on me, they're too boxy, my body gets lost in the shape. And Curls, I laughed, what about Arab men looking for wives with that Madonna-whore complex of theirs? She laughed, said she was dating a Jew, a cis man, her words again, I would never say such a ridiculous thing. Thinking of Sasha, I asked her if I could bring my own pet male. Sure, if he's rich, she laughed. As we talked, I continued watching the brunette correspondent on Sofia's TV, behind her the White House. I liked doing several things at once, it calmed me.

The day before winter break, I brought Trenchcoat to my classroom. Sasha had been begging me to meet the students but I didn't want them to be inspired by his self-effacing humility, so I brought Trenchcoat instead. They were young boys, they wanted to talk to girls and be alphas, so I needed to build their confidence.

I had prepared the students in advance, I told them that Trenchcoat was a fashion sensei and taught children in Monaco. You know, I said to them, a six can easily become an eight with the right manners and clothing, it's not the same for women, you're lucky to be men. They didn't understand what I was talking about, their faces were blank. There will be no writing assignment, I said, it's a free class, do what you want with it.

It sounds like I was running a circus at Franklin, but most of my teaching was very sober and serious. Children spend a lot of time at school, I had them for hours and hours each week, and there was only so much entertainment that I could come up with. I'm telling you about the fun times, but trust me that in between there was plenty of reading and writing.

It wasn't easy getting Trenchcoat into Franklin. Americans are very protective of their children, maybe because it's the only country in the world with the cultural practice of school shoot-ings. So I had to tell Lauren, the receptionist, to register Trench-coat as a guest lecturer from Syria, a member of the New York Refugee Action Committee, which was something I invented, al-though I'm sure it exists in real life as well.

That morning, Trenchcoat woke up early, he bathed for a long time and ironed his uniform twice. He insisted that we take a taxi to Franklin, because it was raining melted glaciers, a type of rain that flooded subway stations in New York, and he was afraid we'd be late.

We got there early, Trenchcoat stood at the doorway of my classroom and shook hands with each of the eighth graders as they walked in, introducing himself politely, bowing, as if he were hosting the World Economic Forum. The students all formed a line outside the classroom, waiting for their turn to shake his hand. At first they awkwardly blurted out their names, but then some made eye contact, shook hands more firmly, introducing themselves by their full names. They all sat at their desks, calmly, there was not one student fidgeting in his seat.

Trenchcoat stood at the front of the room, took off his trench coat, hung it on the back of my desk chair, smoothed his hair back with both hands then unbuttoned his suit jacket. His voice was low, it didn't project, and the boys had to stay quiet to hear him.

Mr. Jenkins, he gestured at Jay, who was sitting in the front row. He asked him to stand up, then he pointed at his jacket, and asked him to please button it. Jay stood upright like a soldier and buttoned his jacket, but Trenchcoat just calmly said to him, No, that's wrong, please unbutton it and sit back down. There was a silence, the students looked at one another, and then at me, I was sitting in the back row. Jay turned around and looked at me with a mixture of hurt and anger, as if I were his mom who had humiliated him in front of his friends. I cleared my throat, before he could say anything, and softly asked him to come sit next to me. Then I gave Trenchcoat a look, letting him know that he had gone too far. Okay, he said to the boys, I will give you the answer. You never button the lower button, only the top one, understand? There was a silence in the room, then Ahmed gasped, and the boys all looked down at their bellies, to see if they had been buttoning their jackets the wrong way.

Trenchcoat explained to them the rules of men's fashion, and he picked Sal as his assistant. They demonstrated how a jacket should fit, the correct length for a pair of trousers, how to pick a collar, how to shine your shoes, and how to wash a white shirt so that it doesn't oxidize. Sal was tall, built, he loved himself and it showed in his clothing.

Then Trenchcoat called on Carl. I worried that Carl was too nervous for this exercise, and too poorly dressed, because he always wore clothes the wrong size, either too large or too small. Carl sluggishly got up from his chair and made his way to the front of the classroom. Alora, Trenchcoat said, Mr. Yu. He hit Carl on the back, Stand straight. Carl straightened up, then looked up at Trenchcoat like a puppy. Your pants are okay at the waist, but they are too long. Trenchcoat then got on the floor, knees and hands on the blue carpet, and explained to them the pant break. He folded Carl's hem, which was wet and grimy from the morning rain, then stood up and told Carl that his jacket was too small, Have you been eating too much rice? he asked. Carl turned red. I wanted to put an end to it but Trenchcoat then pointed at Leonard and asked if he could borrow his jacket, just for the presentation. Leonard obliged, and Trenchcoat dressed Carl in Leonard's jacket, borrowed Sal's oxfords and bowtie, then gave Carl his own handkerchief, watch, and cuff links, which he told the boys come with enormous responsibility, because they're very easy to lose, and it's important to develop the habit of always keeping them in their case, never lying around on the dresser. He gave Carl a final adjustment, told him to lift his chin, close his mouth. Voilà, he announced, presenting Carl to the classroom. The students all clapped for Carl, a show of sympathy that I had never seen before, they were always excessively cruel to him, but perhaps he really did look that good. There was a long mirror in the cupboard behind my desk, and I stood up and opened it so Carl could see himself. He looked at his figure, smiled, then looked himself in the eyes, and I could tell that he liked what he saw.

Class is almost over, I told them. Do you have any final questions? Sal asked if suits could be worn with sneakers, and Trenchcoat answered that it was not possible, under any circumstances. Jay then asked Trenchcoat if he was a homosexual. I suppose it was my fault, because the previous week I had told them that James Baldwin was a homosexual, and that there was nothing shameful about that, it was just a fact of life, and one that often comes with a desirable set of traits, like strong friendships and refined taste. You might be surprised, but Jay asked the question with a straight face, and none of the students giggled or jumped in their seats when he said it.

But this time it was Trenchcoat who turned red. He looked down at the ground, searching for his words, then up at me. I slammed the cupboard door shut and answered for him. Come on, boys. A gentleman doesn't kiss and tell.

At the end of the day, the bell rang, the kids all started jumping up and down, they were off for winter break. It was not yet four in the afternoon and it was already dark outside. Aisha hugged each of them goodbye, telling them not to run because the sidewalks had frozen. I saw Trenchcoat waiting for me across the street and I quickly walked over to him, my CVS basket flailing behind me on the busted asphalt. Aisha saw me with Trenchcoat, I saw her checking him out, top to bottom. I started walking toward the station but Trenchcoat pointed at a yellow taxi.

We have to prepare before going to Paris, he said, putting my basket in the trunk and getting in the passenger seat. I read the driver's name on the placard, it was Gini Ladlock. Where are we going? I asked. Trenchcoat said we were going shopping, and when I asked him where, he said we were going to the ugliest designer in the world. Do you know who it is? he asked, looking back at me through the plastic partition, like a parent posing a question to his child. Vetements, I said. No, he said, firmly, like I had insulted his riddle. Versace? I asked, knowing it to be the wrong answer, because Trenchcoat adored Versace. Gini drove like a maniac up Madison, in a few minutes we were already in midtown. I looked out the window, the Christmas lights and shops rushing by. I was feeling comfortable in my body again, Trenchcoat had given me a painkiller outside school, maybe that's why Aisha had been looking at us. I observed Trenchcoat in the side mirror, his missing molar distended by the view's distortion. I'll give you a clue, he said. Which designer is worn by the richest people in the world, and the poorest people in the world, and it is only the person wearing them who makes the difference? All of them, I laughed. Gucci, LV, Chanel, Prada, Balenciaga, Hermès, Dior. Yes, he said, and Gini braked abruptly. You said it. Now which is the ugliest? The sky was clear but pitch-black, the temperature below freezing. Only a few tourists were out and the shops were brightly lit and empty. We were stopped outside Hermès.

Every year, regardless of poverty, war, or famine, the price of the Birkin bag increases. Its value is more solid than gold or the S&P 500, and the luxury house of Hermès has achieved this by only selling to a very small and particular group of people.

Of course, this is not the explanation Trenchcoat gave me. His was more like, Hermès hates Americans and Asians and they won't sell them any bags, so we, the gorgeous and cultured, would buy the bags and sell them at a premium to the trashy and unworthy. When I inquired further, I realized that it was a scheme, that we would buy the bags and sell them to Ivan, who would meet us every evening at the Mandarin in Paris, and Ivan would sell them to someone else, and so forth, until they ended up in the manicured hands of whichever person had plenty of money but no class.

In Paris there are more bags, Trenchcoat told me as we got out of the taxi, our chances there will be higher, this is just reconnaissance. Surprisingly, there was no doorman, and I had to pull the heavy door myself. We were the only people in the store, there was no music, it smelled good but forced, like the Terre perfume with undertones of mold. We walked around the jewelry, I became aware of the sound my boots made on the marble, I slowed my steps. I thought that we were just browsing, as we had often done, declining champagne. But then Trenchcoat asked the saleswoman to show me some earrings and she took me to a case at the center of the room. She was blond, middle-aged, a non-player, much like Dominic, the waiter at The Mark. Do you like these? she asked me in no accent whatsoever, observing my Birkin from up close, to see if it was real. These earrings are from the Finesse collection. She took the earrings out of the case, the design was very simple, like something I could buy for fifteen dollars at Accessorize. They're simple and clean, Trenchcoat said, I want to buy you earrings. I whispered to him that I didn't have holes in my ears but he ignored me. He picked a pair of rose gold earrings studded with diamonds. I thought I would have to pay with my Mastercard, because I didn't have enough cash, but Trenchcoat pulled out an American Express I had never seen before, with no name on it. Days later, in Paris, I understood that he was building a purchasing history, so that when Hermès looked up his name in their database, they would see that he was a high-spending customer, that he belonged to that very small and particular group of people.

Gini then took us to Select, we sat in the room in the back, and I had four glasses of cognac while Trenchcoat finally lit his dry cigar. We were not pretending anymore. We laughed, very loudly, we spoke to the tables next to us, I reapplied my red lipstick and did not care that it had smeared over my teeth. My speech was wet from the alcohol, maybe I was drooling red. Trenchcoat did not know how to smoke, he burned himself with the cigar and squealed with pleasure.

I can't remember how, but we made it home and I threw myself or was thrown onto the armchair. Trenchcoat took off my shoes, my socks, gave me a glass of water. Are you ready? he asked. For what? He disappeared for a minute, I almost fell asleep but I thought we were finally going to have sex so I forced my eyes open. He came back shirtless, carrying my sewing kit. He then opened the box of earrings, said, Mamma mia, and started blazing two needles with the matches from Select. I held on to his bicep, he held my ear. I trusted him with all my heart that the holes would be symmetrical, the job clean. He pierced the first ear and I wailed, exaggerating the pain, then he quickly moved to the second. He started giggling, but his biceps stayed flexed, controlled, and I moaned while juicy tears slid down my neck. He put the diamonds in me and carried me to bed. The next morning, in the mirror, I looked like more of a woman.

When I was little, I eradicated the entire bottom tier of the crystal chandelier hanging above my parents' bed. They would shower together, even after ten years of marriage. They were very close, very similar, I never heard them fight or argue, and I never heard them have sex. Just a lot of talking, from the head. While they showered, I would enter their bedroom and climb on their bed, a thick, bouncy mattress with a red velvet cover. I would jump, higher and higher, until the tips of my fingers could touch the chandelier, and then I would snap out a jewel in my palm. Some evenings, I would manage two crystals, and I would climb down from the bed, hold the crystals to my ears, looking at myself in the mirror, spraying on some of my father's cologne, pretending to be Marie Antoinette. I didn't know who Marie Antoinette was, I just knew she was a queen, and in my mind, this was good.

We landed in Paris on a Monday morning, just in time for the work-week. I didn't want to leave the hotel so Trenchcoat ordered coffee to our room, something bitter and black in white china, I liked the sound of it touching my teeth, and offered me a Doliprane 1000. He opened the door for a bellboy who had brought back our clothes ironed on plastic hangers. Today will be a great day for you, Trenchcoat said, placing a coin in the boy's palm. It was a two-euro coin, wide and heavy, a golden planet encircled by a silver ring. All week I marveled at the coin's grace, at times I held on to it, hard in my fist, waiting to come by the right person at night, to give it to them with all its powers.

Trenchcoat had packed for me, he was very attached to my clothes, especially the silk items, which the bellboy had brought back glistening and smooth. He had also packed me a pair of Golden Goose sneakers. When I took them out, I was disgusted at having touched them, because they looked dirty and distressed, like they had been worn for five years at least, or for two years by someone who had really lived. They're new, Trenchcoat told me, they make them like this. I read the text on the dust bag, For dream use only, then touched the scuff marks, they were printed.

Are you sure about this? I asked. They don't look very presentable. Trust me, Trenchcoat said, the right people know.

Before we left the hotel room, Trenchcoat instructed me on how to talk to the sales associates at Hermès. The great majority of people are refused a Birkin, they get told that there aren't any available in the store, which is a lie, they just don't want to give it to them. After consultation with Ivan, Trenchcoat decided that the best strategy was to act as natural as possible, because I already owned a Birkin, I already belonged to that very small and particular group of people. What kind of Birkin would you like? Trenchcoat asked me. The same, but smaller, I answered. Very well, he said. When they ask you, say that you would like the same one, but smaller, although between us, any Birkin would do, a Kelly as well. But say you want a Birkin. A woman of your age should know her place in the world, the Kelly is for older women.

Trenchcoat and I entered the elevator. My perfume echoed in the small space, combining with Trenchcoat's, which was from a sample of Spice & Wood by Creed. What kind of woman are they looking for? I asked. Someone elegant, he answered, looking at my reflection in the mirror. Hold your mother's Birkin firmly but casually. Like it's small change for you, but like every cent counts.

We left the hotel, in our uniforms, and started walking up Rue Saint-Honoré. All week the weather was oppressive, like we were living in a beautiful old house with low ceilings. Ordinary people looked good, and it wasn't some great cultural triumph, it was just that the high street shops sold nicer clothes. There was no Target, no Walmart, no Macy's, and therefore no mixing of colors, and hardly any prints. Shapes were sleek, and, perhaps most importantly, bodies were slim. It's the surest way to make a piece of clothing look good, or to make a person look good in general.

I felt calmer there, and I understood, for certain, that I was doomed to fail in America, that the family curse would apply to

me as well. I was too selfish to stick out the years before I'd qual-
ify for a green card.

Yes, you're right. Everybody in my family was selfish. Even
when they died, they did it selfishly, ensuring that their interests
would live on. You too, you're selfish. You could have left but you
decided to stay. You could have been quiet, but you keep asking
questions.

When we entered the store nothing caught my eye. There
were belts with *H* buckles, bracelets with *H* clasps, sandals with
H vamps, and the iconic bags and scarves of course. I found it
all very boring and banal. I looked down at my shoes, then up
at Trenchcoat, wondering what was next. You're not supposed to
look down, he whispered to me. From now on, you only look up,
or higher, never down. If you have to look at something, do it from
the corner of your eye, never show enthusiasm.

Trenchcoat knew exactly where to go, and we found the receptionist on the second floor, standing by the horse saddles. He
gave her his name, and she looked him up on her list. We had an
appointment for four in the afternoon, but Trenchcoat had told
me that only one or two Birkins were sold in the store each day,
and we would have a better chance if we came earlier, although
not too early, because they had to reject some customers before
anything else. The whole model was based on rejection, people
want to belong to a club that doesn't accept them. It was only
noon, but we pretended this was the correct time of our appointment, and the receptionist pretended we were right.

We waited for a few minutes, and then a sales associate named
Charlie came and took us to a private room in the back. I saw the
eyes of the other customers following us, wondering if we'd be
successful. The store was full of people, young and old, mostly
women, of all nationalities. I had the feeling that the great majority of them were after the same thing as us, a Birkin or a Kelly,

and that a non-negligible number, especially the young girls all alone, were part of the same scheme.

Charlie asked me what I wanted and I answered him, A Birkin, in black, gray, or bleu nuit, I don't wear much color in general. I answered like I was a bit bored, like his concern was burdening me, like he was my maid asking me what I would like for lunch. And to my surprise, Charlie, with his small eyes and hands, did not obey my call to servitude. Instead, he answered back in the same currency, looking bored by me, by my looks, as if I were the burden, as if my natural beauty were invisible to him. He pointed at my mother's Birkin and said I already had one. Yes, I said, but this one is too large. I suppose one can never have too many Birkins? he asked. But I just looked away. It must be a test, I thought, only a vulgar woman would agree to such a statement. He then turned to Trenchcoat and told him that there weren't many Birkins around, that the stock opens at unexpected hours, but he would go and check. I changed strategy, and instead of fighting back, I gave him a coy smile. I thought, If anyone is going to score this bag, it's going to be Trenchcoat, not me. I'm here as an accessory, I'm Trenchcoat's Finesse collection.

Charlie came back with a big orange box. Inside was a gray Picotin handbag. The Picotin was cylindrical, with an open top that was squeezed shut with a thin strap and a padlock. I suppose it was inspired by horses' feed buckets. Try it, Trench-coat said, not flinching, implicitly instructing me how to react. Charlie unboxed the bag and put it in my hands. It was not the Birkin, it was lighter and more supple, but it also had feet. I hung it on my left forearm and looked at myself in the mirror. I had dark circles under my eyes, the Golden Goose sneakers made me look boyish, the silk pants had already wrinkled around my crotch. The bag was dead to me, like something sold in the stalls on Fifth Avenue and Fourteenth Street, but Trenchcoat was smiling euphorically. I forced myself to look at the bag, to feel something. I switched sides and hung it delicately on my right arm. I touched the handles like they were precious, as precious as the hands of children. I like it, I said. I couldn't fake a smile with my eyes open so I closed them and made childish dolphin noises. What do you think? I asked Trenchcoat. Everything looks great on you, he answered, but I wanted to get you something more formal, this is good for every day. Then Trenchcoat looked at Charlie, asked him what he thought. Charlie said that the Picotin was an elegant and timeless bag, something of that sort, and it was the right size for me. Then he asked Trenchcoat what he did for a living, and Trenchcoat told him, I'm an art dealer, a bit like you. Out of politeness, Charlie asked me what I did. I looked in the mirror and told him I was an actress, mostly children's theater. After that, we sat on the couch, we got to know Charlie, we accepted the champagne. Every detail he revealed, the country of his birth, which was Belarus, his immigration, his dream of becoming a shoe designer, brought him closer to our hearts and lower to our feet.

Eventually Trenchcoat looked at his Rolex and told me that it was already three o'clock. He gave Charlie his number and asked him if he would like to join us for dinner. As I was getting ready to leave, Trenchcoat gave it one last shot. Was it possible that the stock had opened while we were talking, Monsieur, could you check for a Birkin, it would make this young woman very happy. Let me check, Charlie said. Madame, do you have a minute? The minutes rolled by, I felt my stomach turn, I was hungry. But then Charlie came back with a small black Birkin, size 20. Trenchcoat very quickly pulled out fourteen thousand two hundred and seventy euros in cash from my mother's Birkin, the size 35, and said, We'll also take the Picotin, why not. I don't know where the cash came from. It wasn't, and then it was, and then it wasn't again.

Charlie asked for my passport and registered the Birkin and Picotin under my name.

In the taxi I fell asleep in Trenchcoat's lap. At the hotel, the handbags stayed downstairs in the lobby with Trenchcoat. When he came up, I was already underneath the covers, flipping through the television channels. He showed me the thick stack of green bills and put it in the hotel safe. Tomorrow we'll go to George V, he said, it will be easier there, Ivan knows someone. I nodded, already absorbed by the screen, then I ordered steak tartare from room service and watched a porn star being interviewed on CNN.

At George V, I got a baby blue Kelly and a small Constance with a golden buckle, which I learned would be more profitable for us than the palladium. The store manager, Paul, was bribed by Ivan, and when we entered the store, Paul greeted us like we were old friends. Oh, it's so great to see you again. Until when are you here again. How is it going this year. I saw some sketches of the new line, fantastic.

While they spoke, I examined my reflection in the mirror, from the side, following Trenchcoat's instructions. My new earlobes were swollen, a bit red. I wondered how I'd gone half a lifetime never wearing earrings, what a waste. I looked more feminine in them, they softened my features. I knew that there were other things, many things, that I could do to look more beautiful. These days, even the most hideous monsters can become desirable with the right makeup and surgery. I resented this, of course, because it was unfair to women who possessed natural beauty. And yet I knew that if I were to be truly natural, unwashed, and unshaved, I would be untouchable, unbearable to look at.

The night before, Trenchcoat had taken me to a photo booth in the Concorde metro station and then immediately delivered the photos to Ivan. The next morning, he appeared with more cash and a fake passport, thin and flimsy, from the Republic of Armenia. Trenchcoat scheduled the appointments at Hermès under his name and registered the bags under mine. I needed a new passport, though, to not arouse suspicion. Trenchcoat said that I'd get a new passport for each bag, but not to get too excited, because these passports were not good enough for becoming a fugitive, only for buying handbags.

Paul asked me what I was after and I ran through my script. It was effortless and in no time Trenchcoat pulled out eighteen thousand euros and that was that, I had the Kelly and the Constance, registered with my Armenian passport. When we exited the shop, Trenchcoat started skipping and dancing around the boulevard. He had invited Paul for dinner, and I was sure that Paul was gay, his pelvis gave it away, it tilted backward. Just as I thought that, Trenchcoat nearly got hit by a seven-seater Peugeot. I need a hot shower, I told him, and he understood what I meant. I wasn't keeping up with my rituals, I had been neglectful. I was becoming like the filthy and rich, a fishy pussy with a floral neck.

I walked alone to the hotel, crossing a row of furniture shops. It was the magic hour, when the stores closed and plazas transformed into homeless camps. They were not like the homeless of New York, they were migrant workers. Some fifty men and women were spreading their tents and sleeping bags along the storefronts. Their hair was clean, their sleeping areas were tidy. Some of them were already cozy, watching the screens of their smartphones. Others were having dinner, canned and packaged. Behind them, sofas and beds were lit in the display windows. There was a small group of men on folding chairs, chatting in a language, I suppose it was Eastern European. They looked like the middle-aged men of some provincial town, chitchatting, feeling at home. I crossed the street, it was theirs now.

I walked down an alley, then took a left, passing by a park with a large bronze statue. On the gate of the park was a big sign and just two words, in English, SQUARE CLOSED. It reminded me of the locked park across from my apartment in New York.

I had my shower and I got into bed but there was a word that I had caught from the men's conversation, *molya*. It had gotten stuck to my tongue. I kept hearing the man's voice in my head, and he reminded me of Sasha.

I picked up the phone and called him, but there was no answer. I suspected that he hadn't taken it well, my affair with Trenchcoat, but that he wouldn't admit it. I wrote him a long message explaining that Trenchcoat and I hadn't even kissed. There is nothing between us, I wrote, it's purely recreational. The next day Sasha called me, very casually. I invited him to the gala that Curls was organizing in February. Sasha had a lot of money, more money than me, and I wanted to steer him in the right direction, I wanted him to do something good with his money, other than wiring it to his dysfunctional family in Russia. And I wanted something else from him, I had a dream that he would lend me the facade of that building on Fifth Avenue, just for a week or so, and let me put up a billboard and say and show whatever I wanted there. But on a personal level, on a romantic level, I had no respect for Sasha. I knew that I would continue to betray him, I just didn't know for how long.

At the Hermès near Lutetia we were treated well, I was given a chair to sit in while we waited, and Trenchcoat discussed the store's design with the receptionist. They walked along the edge of the floor, pointing at materials, like they were explorers in nature, naming the flora and fauna. I watched the women in the store, and I had the impression that they were real customers, the French women were older and alone, the foreign women were accompanied by men. Judging by their complexion and style, they were foreigners from exotic countries, rich wives and daughters from failed states, banana republics, and friendly dictatorships. Their style was different, extroverted, heavy on the bling and makeup. It said we may be terrorists or crooks or gangsters, but at least we have pride, and we smell fantastic.

In the corner of the store, near the porcelain, I saw one young woman, blond, very slender, carrying a Louis Vuitton mini duffel bag. I felt that she was a part of our scheme, that she was my competitor for the day's last Birkin. As I walked by, I fired an arrow of contempt at her, to make her feel small, so that she would fail in her performance.

At last, the salesman came, and he was very transparent, his body flexible, he wasn't holding tightly to his character like the other sales associates. He was Malaysian, with taught, maple skin and long lashes. His name was Mubarak. He had just become a French citizen, he said, and his friends wanted to go to the Pride parade in Tel Aviv, but he was still hesitant. I told him I was Palestinian and had just become a citizen of Armenia. Sometimes, maybe even most of the time, telling a stranger that you're Palestinian is a handicap, it makes people withdraw from you, it makes them unsure or suspicious. But other times it's like showing a hand of four aces. You get a pat on the back, you get Yasser Arafat's *V* sign, you get free stuff. And that day, when I told him, Mubarak sold me a size 35 Birkin in crocodile skin, the color of ganache. Happy Pride, Vive la Palestine, Eid Mubarak.

We went to celebrate at the Lutetia hotel bar. Trenchcoat ordered for us, since he was a man of languages and naturally esteemed by servers. There was a couple at the bar, sitting on high chairs, colleagues maybe, playing naive. The man had smooth hair and a mole on his chin. The woman kept looking at my Hermès shopping bag, sitting on the chair next to me, then at Trenchcoat.

The wine arrived, and it wasn't to Trenchcoat's taste. He argued with the server, told him that it was not what he'd ordered and that the glass smelled of bleach. But the server couldn't understand what Trenchcoat was saying. It occurred to me then that Trenchcoat's French was not good, that there was no accord between how he held himself and who he really was. Even the woman at the bar looked away in embarrassment.

Yes, Trenchcoat's company was a celebration, but things were beginning to shift between us. He began to take weight, to get heavy, he was stirring some feelings in me and they were making me tired.

No, I'm not tired of you. Not yet. There is still something material between us, I still have things to say. But in the end, I will get tired. Or I will get bored and I will end it.

Back in our hotel room, Trenchcoat went to see Ivan in the lobby, and when he came back, he took his eye cream out from the minibar, not even offering me any, patting it on his eyelids with his middle finger, which I thought was very rude. He said he was going to dinner again with Paul. Did you invite Mubarak? I asked. When he said no, I said I wasn't coming either.

I knew that Europeans like Paul were racist and that they looked down on people like us. It was only one glorious summer in the sixties and my expensive clothes that made them act otherwise. I knew this because I felt the same about Mexicans, Native Americans, Ukrainians, Africans, and all kinds of East and South Asians. The racial hierarchy is not dichotomous. These Europeans could kiss my ass with their fine hypocrisy.

While Trenchcoat was out, after I had finished off the minibar, I went to get a drink in the hotel lobby. The bar was closing, the Eiffel lights went out, and I told this bald man all kinds of lies. I'm a geologist, I told him, I specialize in seashells, and now I mostly make jewelry and bespoke furniture. I then told him my mother was sleeping upstairs so it would be best to go to his room, where I poured a shot into my throat and chased it with his fat dick. It smelled good, and I didn't want him to finish. I didn't want him at all actually, I just wanted his organ. I didn't even catch his name because he had terrible diction, I think it was Kurt.

In the morning, Trenchcoat met me in the lobby for breakfast, his white shirt completely open except for one button. The gentle patch of hair on his chest was showing, and at certain angles, you could see his nipples in bold italics. When I saw this, I took him back upstairs and changed into my Simone Rocha shirt without a bra, so people could see my nipples too.

Paris was extroverted, men and women of all ages were very easy. The only ones who exuded sex in New York were the street people, and when I say *street people* I mean those people who live on the street but don't sleep there. They hang around and call you names and it's all quite petty. They say cheesy thing like, I want your smile. My smile is yours, you answer, have it forever. After that, they try to kiss you and you walk away. I could never hate them for that.

I told Trenchcoat what I had done the night before, so he understood that he was not the only man in my life. He was circumcised, I said, even though I couldn't remember.

I suffer from sexual amnesia. I can never remember the details, or what was said and done. It's a blissful blank for me, like the deep hours of sleep. I cease to exist.

The day before Christmas, we went back to the flagship store in Saint-Honoré, and that's when everything started to go wrong. My impatience had previously served us well, it appeared as if my time was worth more, and I could see that people were threatened. But when I waited more than ten minutes, I imitated the tone of the sales associate, Cecile, back at her and I told her, I'm a fifty thousand–euro customer, offer me a glass of water and a Doliprane 1000. But she was an even bigger bitch than I was, she said I had no record at the store, that she had never seen me before. Trenchcoat then got angry, he demanded to look in the database, he wanted to see the manager, but the manager was her. I suddenly looked at him, at his face, at his body, and I saw someone ugly. His mouth was mangled, his chest was puffing, looking larger than the rest of his body, and he started to call Cecile names, in different languages, and all those names had something to do with her being a woman. For the first time, Trenchcoat and I left the store empty-handed.

Ivan booked us a train to London immediately, before we could get blacklisted internationally. He put a lot of pressure on us, the stores would soon close for Christmas, and he needed bags, many bags, he even agreed to double our commission. I was ready to give up, I could no longer understand why we were turning ourselves into beggars, but Trenchcoat wanted to keep going.

It would have been unfair to stop him from making money. It looked like our assets were shared, but we both knew that the bottom line was still there, beneath the performance.

He took my phone and dialed a foreign number. I didn't know he spoke Spanish but it didn't surprise me. He could have been a Latino for all I knew, which would mean that although I'd never been in the home of a Latino, a Latino had been in mine. Trenchcoat had never told me where he was from. When I asked him at the airport, noting his passport was red, he said that his life project was to be from nowhere and everywhere. I snapped the red passport from his hand, but it was Dominican, which didn't mean anything, because the Dominican Republic was known for its citizenship schemes.

After he finished the call, he told me that he had spoken to a director at Hermès in London, that he would meet us there and get us whichever bag we wanted. I'm not going, I told him, I've had enough of Hermès, it's humiliating. I'm not like you, I said, I don't need to pretend. He stayed calm, told me he was going to go alone and would be back in time for our dinner reservation. Sure, I said, but for fuck's sake, it's Christmas Eve tonight, it's a set menu.

I walked back to the hotel, and I wondered if it was true, what I had told him, that I didn't need to pretend. Maybe pretense was all there was. Fashion is pretense, education is pretense, personality, too, is a form of internalized pretense. I wondered what my true essence would be, if I were solitary, in nature, untamed and unconditioned.

spent the rest of the day in the hotel bed, watching TV and ordering room service. They didn't have what I was craving, so I asked for all the side dishes, which were a green salad, fries, spinach, creamed leeks, and ratatouille, and I ate them all with bread and butter like they were meze. I was so lost in the haze of food and CNN, I barely noticed that it was already dark out. Trench-coat texted me that he was on his way back to Paris, that he had bought a limited-edition Kelly with a pocket on the outside, and that he would meet me at La Closerie des Lilas at eight.

I called room service again, ordered a tarte tatin, and got dressed very quickly. I had bought myself a new Dior eyeshadow palette, a Christmas gift to myself, and I tried on all the colors on my eyelids, first one by one, and then I mixed them all together, while I finished off the dessert and the minibar absinthe.

I stepped out of the hotel, the night was cold and windy, I wrapped my Loro Piana scarf around my head and ears, not like Grace Kelly in a convertible but like a hijabi in Islamopho-bic France. I thought that the streets would be full of women in lavish dresses, fathers carrying gifts, and little boys in tuxedos, but I saw none of that, only lone men with hands in their pock-ets, walking quickly. I should have taken a taxi, but I decided to walk, and then, realizing how unpleasant the wind was, it was constantly changing directions, pushing me forward, then pushing against me, I headed for the metro station.

I entered at Concorde, where the previous week I had taken the photos for my fake passports. I bought a ticket at the machine, then descended the stairs to the platform. It was completely deserted. The train would arrive in six minutes. The walls of the Concorde station were covered with letters, like Scrabble tiles, and I started searching for words while I waited. I suppose it was some kind of mural or gimmick. I scanned the wall on the other side of the platform, and I found a few words, in English even, like *trouble, quiet, republic*. When I turned around to scan the wall behind me, I looked down, and I saw a man sprawled on the platform. He was dark, famished, curled up on the ground, his eyes closed. He wasn't wearing a shirt, no shoes either. I looked around, there was no one there but us, the train would arrive in five minutes. I took a step toward him, just one step. I saw that he was in fact a handsome man, but the way he was lying reminded me of a dog. I tried to get closer, but I couldn't, I was too afraid.

I walked back up the stairs of the station, no one was there, and no one was coming. I thought about leaving, I could walk the remaining distance to the restaurant, where Trenchcoat was surely waiting for me, in a festive mood. But I went back down to the platform, and the man was still there, lying silently. For a while, I tried to approach him, to see if he was breathing, but my feet wouldn't let me. I tried waking him up, but my voice was too low.

The train came, and I stepped inside and took a seat in front of the window, looking at the man on the floor. Just then, a policewoman entered the platform from one end, a middle-aged Black woman. From the other end of the platform, another policeman entered, an old white man, the tunnel wind swooshing back his silver hair. The doors of the train closed, we started moving. The two police intercepted, they greeted each other with a kiss, white cheek on Black cheek, the dog body below.

I nside the train, an older woman was seated in front of me, wearing a little red dress underneath a long black coat. She was the same age as my neighbor Sofia but her hair was long, blond, pulled up in a bun to reveal a freckled neck. Her shoulders were caving in, I could see the V of her thighs touching the metro seat, which in Paris was upholstered. I could tell that she had had a beautiful body, once, and that this identity hadn't left her with old age. I thought she was very put together, and this soothed me.

The train came to an abrupt stop and she lost her balance slightly, causing me to look down at her feet. I only saw it for a second, and quickly I looked away. She was wearing bordeaux leather heels, open-toed although it was winter, with a thin strap and a little golden buckle around the ankle. The heel itself was high, wooden, tapering to a sharp point. A nice shoe, if not my taste. But inside the shoe, her feet looked ancient, thick, crusted with a layer of broken skin, the heel dry and rocky, yellowing and gray.

Something collapsed inside my stomach, I looked again at her feet. Her toenails were long and thick, it appeared as if a long time ago she had applied some red polish but they since had grown, each in a different direction, and the toes themselves were merging into one mass. Pardon, she said to me, pointing at the floor. I flinched, but it was only my wallet, it had fallen out of my Birkin. I picked it up in a hurry and jumped out at the next station. I texted Trenchcoat that I wasn't coming to dinner. He would do just fine alone at Closerie, ordering his meat well done, sitting across from a prestigious orange shopping bag.

I had only managed a few seconds of looking at her feet but speaking to you now, I can see them as if they are in front of me, I can smell the metro platform, the angel of death approaching through the dark tunnel. In her disgusting feet I could see those faces that appear in the roots or hollows of ancient olive trees.

On my way back to the hotel, I bought a baguette and jamón at a Franprix and walked toward the locked park. The homeless camp was no longer there, maybe they were home for Christmas. The wind had intensified, everything was in motion, only the bronze statue was anchored and still. I got closer to the fence of the park, it was clipped and bent, like the fences of Palestine, so I folded my long coat and climbed over it.

Unlike the locked park of New York, this one was taken care of. The bushes were trimmed, the garden itself was geometrical, pruned, the living matter upright and sculpted. I walked around the bronze sculpture, then sat on a stone bench. The wind was moving the gravel, creating ambient shaker music, raising a layer of dust in the air. A tree was shading the moonlight. Its big, circular leaves flipped in the wind, revealing two firm kiwis, like a pair of testicles. I saw that next to the kiwis were several pear trees, then green apples. I walked through the park, following the fruit trees, until I got to a greenhouse.

Inside, the air was still. I heard my footsteps on the gravel, I felt my pores opening in the humid heat. I began to sweat, and I took off my scarf and unbuttoned my jacket. I found there all the fruits and vegetables one can dream of, a miniature Eden at the center of the city. Persimmons, eggplants, tomatoes of all specimens, the bright reds signaling to me from the dark. Oranges, clementines, and chilies. I collected the vegetables and fruits, stuffed herbs in my pockets. Vervain, sage, rosemary, mint, and basil.

Yes, it sounds like I had a fever. You are very down to earth. I like that about you, you don't let me fly too high, you keep me grounded. It's possible that I had a fever, considering that I was spending a lot of time outdoors and that I hadn't brought my hat with me to Paris.

When I left the park, I was approached by a homeless woman with patchy blond hair. She wasn't from the homeless camp, she was a junkie. She came to me frantically, her voice desperate, her pants sagging to reveal a young body distorted by bad health. She wanted money, for her fix. I told her, I don't have any. But I have some food, I said, pointing back at the park, there is a lot of food in there. From my Birkin 35, I gave her two oranges and the package of jamón, of which I had only eaten half. She grabbed it all from my hands and ran in the other direction.

I walked away, checking that my wallet was still with me. And then before I entered the doors of the hotel, I felt someone running behind me. It was the woman again, howling. She came running at me, I thought she was going to tackle me, but then she stopped and handed me the package of jamón. It's opened, she said. I know, I answered, but it's very good, I was just eating it. No, she yelled at me, it's not hygienic. Her eyes were flaring, like I had done something terrible to her. I took the jamón from her and entered the hotel. From behind me I heard her shouting, Donne-le á un Black. I went inside and put the jamón in the mini-fridge, next to Trenchcoat's creams. It was delicious back in the park, but after what she'd said, I could not touch it anymore. It would stay there, getting greasier and greasier, until we checked out.

asked the concierge to deliver a bucket to my room. I was limping, I told him I had hurt myself. It had been a long day, first the rejection at the flagship store, that bitch-whore Cecile, those hours lost in bed, then the platform, Parisian Sofia with the sick roots, and the green delirium in the locked park.

I filled the bucket with hot water and soaked my feet while sitting on the toilet. I sat there and emptied my bowels, until the skin of my feet pruned and I was certain that nothing was left inside of me.

In the shower I scrubbed my feet with lava pumice, then brushed them with tea tree soap. I used a softer brush for my vagina, another for my asshole. I covered myself from the neck down with jojoba peeling cream and lay on the five-star marble with my feet propped against the wall, the water shooting between my legs. My knees bent, I rocked my body against the marble, exfoliating the skin of the asymmetrical square on my Turkish hammam loofah. The EGR Game, the patent leather, the controller's ass, the kiss, the proud junkie, it had been a long day, but there I was, cleansing, taking things into my own hands. I moved the lever with my right foot, hotter, then with my left foot, a flash of ice, feet against the marble, brown beads on alabaster, and then,

then the obvious, genitals, dirty, wet genitals, the sounds of their frantic smacking, followed by just three feeble pulses. I opened my eyes and rinsed. I wore slippers from the shower to the bed. Trenchcoat came back late at night. He opened and closed the safe, then sat on the chair by the desk. He took off his shoes, first he inserted the wooden shoe trees, then he took off his socks, wiped his shoes with them, and threw them in the garbage underneath the desk. Ever since he started making money, socks had become disposable to him.

Do you want a foot massage, I asked. I told him to shower first, and I began to massage his slender feet, there is no other way to describe them than to say that they were perfect, that I wanted to put them in my mouth, suck on the toes, bite them, choke on them. I began to kiss his feet, first playfully, lovingly, four or five kisses in a quick row, like he was my baby. Mia amore, he said, giggling. Then I kissed them again, slower, wetter, and when I raised my head to tie my hair up, I wanted to give him a blow job, he said, I'm not attracted to women, it's not your fault, please don't be upset.

After that night, I began to resent his feet, his beauty, his feminine delicacies. I was jealous, it wasn't fair that he got to be both man and woman, that he took from us and didn't give back. It was cultural appropriation.

I came back from Paris determined to fix the printer. It was a Sunday night in January. Fort Greene was quiet, cars were still passing below my apartment but with their windows rolled up. I unpacked my bag, separated the laundry, then started fiddling with the printer.

Trenchcoat heard me from the bedroom, and he came to help. Since that day with Cecile and the foot massage, I'd been very cold to him. He couldn't speak French, I told him, and he was dragging me to a life of beggary. But Trenchcoat was patient with me, steady in the face of my insults. In fact, he became even more helpful.

The way I thought of it, I was a million dollars and Trenchcoat was my wallet. He took care of me, contained me, kept me safe. I knew that I had no time to waste, losing Trenchcoat would be foolish, it was in my best interest to have someone in this world.

Yes, I had Sasha, but Sasha was the past, with Trenchcoat every day was Times Square.

Trenchcoat told me to step aside, he moved the printer to the kitchen, reloaded the ink cartridge next to the stove, and plugged it in. He opened it and blew gently into the crevice, until a tiny piece of paper flew out, like confetti. There was a strange noise, like something straining, a pop, and then a faint percussion of plastic being tickled. It was printing.

Trenchcoat went back to the laundry and I stood there by the kitchen window while the printer worked, watching the homeless man, the one I told you about long ago, who I had wanted to kill with the printer. I watched him, doing nothing, just being. Now I wished that I knew his name, I really did, I walked past him every day like he was a piece of dog shit drying in the sun. Pages came out, from September. It was a peaceful poem by Frank O'Hara. I read the poem again, it said something about me, about what kind of person I was, what kind of teacher I wanted to be for my students. That poem, with all its references to art, was meant to be a vacation from their burdens. There was a moment, before, when I was carefree, when I offered my students lightness. As Frank O'Hara wrote, It seems they were all cheated of some marvelous experience.

The next day, Aisha told me about The Dandies. We were sitting in her office, I had a free hour before lunch, all the boys were in class, and the school was very quiet. She told me that students from the eighth grade had emailed her over winter break, asking for her permission to do a bake sale. They want to fundraise for the New York Refugee Action Committee, she told me, reading the name of the organization from a yellow sticky note. I could hear the sound of the radiators, whirring at full force. It had been an extremely cold weekend, and a pipe had even frozen and burst in the chemistry lab.

You have connections at the New York Refugee Action Committee, don't you? she asked. I nodded, yes, and said I would help the students with pleasure. Aisha was wearing a fleece dress, a piece of clothing I had never seen before nor envisioned existed. It hugged her large form, making her look like an enormous stuffed animal, with her firm, freckled cheeks. I was half her weight and I couldn't wear what she wore.

I asked which students had emailed her, and she said Leonard and Sal. I didn't know they were friends, I said. Me neither, she said, they signed the email as The Dandies.

When Leonard walked into my classroom after lunch, I saw

that his hair was buzzed, it was the end of his bowl cut. He was also wearing a bowtie, as opposed to his usual red kipper, and he had taken a seat in the third row, next to Sal.

It was strange to me, Sal and Leonard didn't belong together. Leonard was gifted and hardworking, whereas Sal had no interest in learning and only wanted to socialize and mess around. But I knew that teenagers could change very quickly, especially over school breaks, they could grow ten centimeters, they could lose their virginity, they could start smoking weed, or they could discover that they were gay.

At the end of class, I called Leonard and Sal over to my desk. Leonard said his mother would do the baking. Tell her to only make brownies, I said, there is no point in selling anything else. I told them I would talk to the Refugee Action Committee and that we'd set a date in a few weeks. They were disappointed that they had to wait so long, but I thought it was better that way, I wanted to see if their friendship would last. And how come you're both wearing bowties? I finally asked. We're The Dandies, Sal said, grinning, pulling his collar. We're bringing you the finer things in life.

I laughed, they were funny, they reminded me of a club I had created with my friend when I was little, we called it PKK, although we knew nothing of the Kurdish resistance group then. Who else is in The Dandies? I asked. We're a very small and exclusive group, Sal answered.

After they left, I saw that Jay was still sitting at his desk, he had heard the conversation, and I could tell he wanted to be a part of it. We cleaned the classroom together, I handled the vacuum cleaner, and at some point, I dropped a twenty-dollar bill on the floor. I thought he would pocket it, but he chased me outside the classroom and tried to give it back. Oh, I said, it's not my money, Jay, keep it for yourself, lucky you.

News of The Dandies spread quickly among the boys. They were always together, and after school they dispatched in small groups to their respective boroughs. Jay and Leonard were from Queens, Sal from Harlem, Reg, Ahmed, and Elijah from Brooklyn. Sometimes I would see them on the R train, Reg would play video games on his phone and Ahmed would draw, a thin piece of paper in his lap, the sharpened pencil poking holes in it. Carl was from Chinatown, he took the bus. Felix from Staten Island, I don't even know how he got back and forth, perhaps that was why he was always running around like a maniac. There were other students, of course, and I cared for all of them. I would have given them my life, if it was possible.

Over the weeks, Leonard and Sal's friendship only got stronger, and more students joined The Dandies. I saw them in their bowties, sitting around Sal's desk during break, leaving school together. I realized that they had been influenced by Trenchcoat, because Jay told me that they were naming each other after tie knots, so Sal was Batwing and Leonard was Bogart, and they all dreamed of buying cuff links.

Meanwhile, Trenchcoat continued with his business venture, he bought all the bags he could get at Hermès in New York, and then started going to other designers, mostly to Louis Vuitton and Gucci, buying whatever limited edition he could find, making small sums of money. We were not sleeping together, so I went back to sleeping with Sasha, when I felt like it.

It was a cold January, a few weeks had gone by with hardly any sunshine, and I tried to teach the eighth graders some poems by Frank O'Hara, to lighten the mood. But they didn't like him, and in the middle of one lesson I got very frustrated, I shouted at them and left the classroom, slamming the door behind me. Jay and Ahmed immediately came after me, told me they were sorry. I was moody, I gave them a hard time. They went back inside and persuaded their classmates to sing for me. Choruses of Sorry, Sorry, Sorry, with Sal dropping Gucci Gang in between.

I went back inside and stood there in silence. I'm sorry too, I finally said, I didn't mean it, I thought you would like these poems. Jay said that the poems were too hard. I said, You need to push yourself harder, Jay, there are no discounts out there in the real world, even if you see a three-for-the-price-of-one at Walmart you should know that it's a scam. Carl was suppressing a mean smile, maybe he'd been laughing at my outburst. I told them they could do whatever they wanted now, We're continuing as a free class. Art is about taste, and taste is formed by experience, I said. Don't ever let anybody dictate your taste, it's as absurd as someone dictating your memory.

Thankfully, Leonard was still an excellent student, and he stayed focused on the poetry, answering all my questions. At the end of that month, he even won the New Year competition. I instructed them to write an essay, predicting what would happen the following year. They could predict anything, I gave them carte blanche. They could predict the weather, the politics, even what would happen in their family and personal lives. I had initially designed the competition hoping that Carl would win, because the prize was a pair of Beats headphones, but Carl was an ingrate, he didn't even submit an essay, and I had to judge the competition fairly and award the headphones to Leonard.

Leonard had written that the school was too poorly managed, the building's infrastructure was falling apart, especially the plumbing, and so Franklin would have to close its doors before the end of the year.

Of my twenty plants, three did not survive winter. The asparagus fern, once like an expansive wing of green feathers, began to shed beige wisps all over the counter and floor. I could not withstand the sight of my failure, its death was taunting me, so one day I grabbed the ceramic pot by its base and hit it upside down into the biowaste container. The fern fell in, the dry stems crushing against rotting egg shells, clementine peels, a cabbage core.

The fate of the pothos vine was different, because I didn't mean to do it. It was hanging on a shelf by the kitchen window, it was a healthy plant, independent, its long vines always touched the crown of my head whenever I looked out at the locked park or tried to listen to the casual arguments at the B67 stop. One day, I grabbed a handful of the vines, to see if they were dusty. I thought I was being gentle, but they ripped, falling to the ground.

The third plant was a palm. It sat there in the corner, all winter, it survived, but I had no love for it. One evening, I carried it down the stairs of my building and left it out on the curb. The next morning, it was gone. Someone took it in, someone managed to love it and keep it, or someone managed to love it and kill it, that was always an option.

The rest of my plants survived, and I tended to them with great devotion. Every week I did my rounds, poking my finger in the soil, dusting the leaves, cutting the yellowing stems, peeking underneath to see if roots were poking out of the drainage holes.

I knew about lonely people who treated their pets like they were children, I'd seen them in my neighborhood, dogs in yellow raincoats and red boots trotting smugly around the homeless like little Ronald McDonalds. Not much differentiated my obsession from theirs, except perhaps that my pets could show neither gratitude nor rebellion, they were utterly under my control. Which is why when I later decided to do away with them, the massacre was silent.

We decided to hold the bake sale on Valentine's Day, it was a business decision. The boys figured they could also sell roses, which Trenchcoat delivered to Franklin at lunchtime, in a plastic blue bucket. All afternoon, the brownies and roses waited in the staff room, and fifteen minutes before the end of the day, I dismissed The Dandies from my classroom and told them to go set up.

There were five trays, twenty brownies in each tray, displayed on a stand at the entrance to Franklin. By the time the bell rang and I went to see them downstairs, they had already sold two trays. Jay had finally managed to buy a bowtie and join The Dandies, and he had made two cardboard signs, one with the name of the charity and the other with a price list. I gave them my Venmo handle so no one would say that they didn't have cash, took one brownie for myself, without paying, then convinced Sal to cut the remaining pieces in half and sell them for the same price.

I stood in a sunny corner nearby, eating the cold, salty brownie, making sure the East Village weirdos stayed away from the boys. Sal handled the cash, Leonard the brownies, Jay the roses. The other Dandies stood in the street, in their bowties and winter puffer jackets, charming the passersby. In less than hour, they were all sold out.

We cleaned up, took the table inside, and Sal handed me the cash. I never gave it to the New York Refugee Action Committee or whatever it was called, because such an organization didn't exist. I can't explain why I behaved that way, it just happened, maybe I didn't believe in organized charity, or I didn't think a couple hundred dollars would make a difference. What mattered was the form, that the students were organizing.

At the end of that week, I called The Dandies to my classroom. The group had continued to grow, they had even recruited some seventh graders. I showed them a printed letter from the president of the New York Refugee Action Committee and told them that he had also sent a gift. Look over there, I pointed. On the windowsill of the classroom, overlooking First Avenue, was a spherical aquarium, inside it were two goldfish. The Dandies stood around the aquarium, poked their fingers in the water. Sal cleared his throat, the others quieted. He said, The small one shall be called Justice, and the one with the fancy tail shall be called Beauty. They all loved the idea, no one dared suggest otherwise.

That evening, Sasha and I went for dinner at a Chinese restaurant, and I held his leg underneath the table. He admired my job, he said it was very important. In general, he liked music, art, children, anything with soul and meaning, since there was none of that in real estate. He dreamed of being a patron of education, or of the arts, although for now he only had some ugly contemporary art hanging in his apartment. Well into the main course, he was still asking about my students, he remembered their names, details about their lives. When he asked me about Jay, I confessed to him that several times now, I had dropped money on the floor while we were cleaning. It wasn't much, maybe twenty dollars at a time.

On the first Monday of March, the teachers all met in the staff room. It was Lauren's birthday, Aisha had baked red velvet cupcakes, and there were also some administrative matters to discuss. The art teacher was going on maternity leave, the second-floor bathroom was totaled, and there was no more budget for athletic activities. I rarely said anything in those meetings, and that day I stayed standing by the windows, with my hands over the radiator, avoiding the calorie bombs. I kept a low profile, I was still a new teacher, and I didn't trust myself to say the right thing.

The last item on the agenda was a letter Aisha had received from some students. She waved the graph paper in the air and said, They're now calling themselves The Movement for Beauty and Justice. She read the letter quickly, it was amusing to her, and she skipped some parts that she didn't understand. They're threatening to go on strike, she continued, they say we have two weeks to respond. She laughed out loud, shook her head. It reminded me of how I had dismissed Carl's suicide note.

Gregory asked which students were behind the letter, and Aisha insisted that it didn't matter, it was a big group, although I think she was trying to protect Sal, because he was her relative.

Can I see the letter? I asked. It was the first thing I had said at the meeting, and Aisha looked at me as if she was surprised to see me there. She handed it to me, it was in Leonard's handwriting, miniature blue. There was a long list of demands, which Aisha had neglected to read. We need a soda machine. We can't do homework on weekends. We want to wear sneakers to school.

What are you going to do about it? I asked, looking around at the teachers, but then looking down at the radiator again, not wanting to seem too invested. Just ignore them, said Gregory, and he started packing his backpack. No, I will not ignore them, Aisha said, we all need to be heard, we can give them something, she continued, maybe a lemonade machine, and we can raise the thermostat temperature to sixty-five.

Aisha belonged to that rare breed of people, kind and gentle people, I think they are born that way. They're more visible in certain professions, in education, or in health care, like the nurses who draw blood. These people often work indoors, they work long, intensive hours, sometimes night shifts. There aren't many of them these days, because our culture socializes us against kindness. I know this because you rarely come across them in the street.

On my way home, a woman stepped onto the train, and though she was a woman there was nothing feminine about her. She was wearing low-rise jeans, a gray hoodie, her hair in a weary braid. I knew that she was going to make a scene, because she entered the train like she was stepping onto a stage.

Good evening, ladies and gentlemen, she started, I'm not asking you for anything, I just want you to listen. Her voice was confident, she paced back and forth in the car, looking at all our faces. I am not a beggar, she said. I'm not a junkie, I don't drink, I don't smoke dope, I don't smoke cigarettes. I recently got out of jail, she said, and then she lowered her voice to add, And if you know, you know. I tried to not look at her, but I couldn't not listen, she was an excellent orator. There are no self-defense laws in New York, she continued, so they charged me with manslaughter. The justice system is whack, she said, and then she added quietly, And if you know, you know. She then appealed to the women on the train, maybe because they're more generous, and said, I'll take any kind of donation, money, food, water, tampons, or feminine hygiene products. I raised my head and asked, Didn't you just say you're not a beggar? But she ignored me, the show must go on, and said, We don't have to be the same color to be sisters.

I snickered, but she continued. I know some of you don't get it, some of you have no idea. She walked right past me, and a woman next to me gave her an apple, which she loudly rejected, showing and telling everyone on the train that she had no teeth but that she'd take an orange instead.

At Canal Street she got off, and another voice started speaking, the voice of a man. Good evening, he said, I'm not a beggar, I'm not homeless, but I've been out of work for a year and I'm just trying to feed my family. He came closer to me, I looked up at him. I'm selling apples and oranges today, he said. One dollar.

For the rest of the ride home, I watched a baby in a stroller being fed mashed food. The baby didn't care about its environment, it just ate it all up, a happy subway baby, for now, although I thought he would surely grow up to be a psychopath.

I got out at the DeKalb stop and stormed the CVS. This branch was full of crazies, the area in which I lived was full of crazies. A lot of train lines intersected there, I told you, as did the Long Island Rail Road. I left the store with a gallon of Clorox on top of the notebooks in the CVS basket. My god, now it struck me. I was an expensive-looking woman, clear skin, glossy hair, wearing a full face of makeup and a floor-length coat and heels. But I was dragging a CVS basket behind me, from Brooklyn to Manhattan, five days a week. What dissonance, no wonder people were looking at me. It was not just my exotic beauty.

The next day, I took the printer with me to school. I arrived a bit late, the sixth graders were waiting for me, seated of course, they were such good boys, and they said nothing about the printer sitting in the CVS basket. During lunchtime, I plugged it in next to Beauty and Justice, and wrote down the instructions on a piece of paper.

When the eighth graders came in, I taught them how to use the printer from their phones. The boys printed all kinds of things, the ink cartridge was mighty. Ahmed printed pictures of his drawings, Jay his class schedule, as well as his brother's. I told them that this was a free printer, there was no limit on how much they could use it or for what purpose. It's a great way to spread your ideas, I said, and after that, The Dandies started printing cryptic signs and posting them around the classroom, with mandates like NO SECOND BUTTON, NO NONSENSE, POST NO BILLS, APRIL 14. Carl was inspired and printed a sign too, DO NOT DISTURB, and taped it to the edge of his desk.

After school, I told Jay that I was very impressed with the letter that was sent to Aisha. Was it you who wrote it? I asked, already knowing that it was Leonard but wanting to compliment him. Everyone had already gone home, it was just us in the classroom, and I was feeding Beauty and Justice while Jay was wiping the desks. I thought about asking Jay to feed the fish, but I was afraid that if they died he would feel responsible.

Jay held my chair while I Windexed the clock. He told me that there was a problem in The Movement for Beauty and Justice. Sal and Leonard had had a fight, Sal said mean things to Leonard, and Leonard wanted to leave the movement, and if Leonard left, Jay would leave too. I asked him when this had happened, I imagined them wrestling in the school corridor or on the subway platform, but Jay told me that it had all happened online. And why did they fight? I asked, still standing on the chair. Sal thinks the letter is stupid, Jay said, and Leonard thinks we should abolish the uniform.

I told him that I didn't think the letter was stupid at all. I told him that the teachers took it very seriously, that they discussed the demands in a meeting, and that they were willing to negotiate. Don't back down, I told Jay, make another threat.

Jay nodded, and a small sound came from his throat, like a hiccup. He took the spray bottle and washcloth from my hand so I could climb down from the chair. I leaned my hand on his shoulder and kissed his forehead.

At the end of that week, my wallet disappeared. It was a Friday afternoon, and I stopped by the CVS next to school to buy cleaning supplies. The First Avenue store was bigger, they carried some brands that my neighborhood branch didn't, like Dettol, which was a favorite for dirty Arabs like me. I could not take my basket inside so I entrusted it to a homeless man with a pit bull, and I told him I'd pay him five bucks upon completion.

In a fresh basket, I piled Lysol wipes, bleach capsules, sponges soft and rough, black shoe shine, and all of the Dettol products I could find. But when it was time to pay, I couldn't find my wallet. Surely I had been robbed. To lose it was not a possibility, I was too organized.

I think my wallet was stolen, I told the cashier. The total was over one hundred dollars. I looked in my 35 again, but there was only my keys, phone, an umbrella, one tablet of Doliprane, and a tube of Cattier. The wallet was gone. Some people were standing in line behind me, they were impatient. Can I take it and pay you tomorrow? I asked, my voice suddenly different, meeker. She rolled her eyes, took my basket, and placed it behind the counter. I loitered around for a bit longer, I thought of shoplifting, CVS was a mega corporation, it was probably the right thing to do, but she kept watching me from the corner of her eye.

It was harder to convince the homeless man and the dog, they wanted their five bucks, but I made a deal with him, Tomorrow I will pay you fifteen. I showed him where I worked. If I don't pay you, I said, you can knock on the blue door and ask for the English teacher.

I swallowed the Doliprane dry and walked home. I kept thinking of the wallet. Where was it? I had last seen it the night before, I had given Trenchcoat some money for a Denver cut. I'd started eating meat again in Paris, it was Trenchcoat's suggestion, he said that meat was suited to my body temperature. The tartare conquered me, and from then on it was meat every day, sometimes for breakfast, lunch, and dinner. My bowel movements changed, my stool was harder. I felt less pure but I had more energy. When the meat was rare, I was up for the fight, I could push my way in the subway, skip lines in cafés, I wasn't ashamed of my aggression. If it was fatty, salty, I felt that it infused me with stamina, I could stay in school for longer, spend more time reading, I had more patience for difficult things.

Halfway across the bridge it began to snow. The snowflakes got bigger, they clung to my Dolce. I walked long stretches without seeing anyone. Night fell and I could barely see ahead of me. By the time I set foot in Brooklyn, the snow was already in piles. My umbrella had flipped inside out, the CVS basket had lost a wheel. I abandoned them both, stuffed the notebooks in my bag, and walked the remaining fifteen minutes with my hands in my pockets, lifting the coat from the inside so the hem stayed dry.

When I got home, I asked Trenchcoat if he'd seen my wallet. He said no, and he asked me if I had seen his cashmere hat, the one he got at The Mark. I despised that hat, and I was glad that it was lost. Easy come, easy go, I told him. He asked if it was me who had made the hat disappear, and this made me very suspicious, I thought that maybe it was he who had taken my wallet.

I looked for my wallet everywhere in the apartment, it was nowhere, it was gone. Trenchcoat didn't help me, he kept looking at himself in the mirror, readjusting his silk handkerchief. He looked good, but he was wearing his shoes inside the house, he was going out in the cold without a hat, and the laundry was still not ironed. Worst of all, I noticed something on the sleeve of his trench coat. I grabbed his arm, looked at it, it was a drop of bleach. Trenchcoat kept telling me to relax. I shouted, he vowed allegiance to me, said the wallet must have fallen from my Birkin, I should really carry a Picotin instead. I slapped myself, and he put his hand to his own cheek and walked out the door. Go, I said, it's snowing, and I know that you are homeless without me. You wear Burberry and Berluti but you're still a hobo. My words rang and rang as I ironed the bedsheets.

When I was nine years old, I opened a bank. I printed a sign with the operating hours, nine to five, and stuck it on the door of my new bedroom in my uncle's house. I had started with a hundred shekels, and on the first day I loaned fifty to my brother and took down his signature in my accounting ledger. The next day, he gave it back to me, plus 10 percent daily interest.

Proud of my entrepreneurial initiative, the whole family started borrowing from my bank. My accounting ledger got longer and longer, I started a dossier. I hid the money in a coffee can in my closet. The can got heavier and heavier, twice a day I would count it and match it with my ledger. I was saving up to buy supplies for a car that I was going to build. I had sketched it out in my notebook and made a list of everything I needed and the estimated price. It was essentially a wooden plank on wheels, with a sail in the front and a portable fan in the back, which was to blow wind into the sail and move the car. My uncle, who was an engineer, explained to me that it wouldn't work, but I insisted, I wanted to build my car. I had a great future ahead of me, they said, I really was my father's daughter.

I managed to save two thousand seven hundred and sixteen

shekels. And then one day in the spring, a friend came over, she was the daughter of an old friend of my father's. My father became successful, his friend didn't, my father died and his friend lived. We had gone on holiday together, the same summer of the accident. Me, my father, my father's friend, and his daughter, in Turkey. During the day we rode jet skis and at night the men drank raki. His daughter was my age, she became my friend, and once or twice a year she would visit me in my new home, my uncle's house. She'd stay over for a few days. We played in the garden, on my bike, climbed the cherry trees. I showed her my doll collection, my Spice Girls album, and my bank.

The morning after she left, my brother came to borrow some money. I pulled out my ledger from the drawer, started a new entry, made him sign. I then instructed him to leave the room. I will be out with the money shortly, I said. I opened the closet, pulled out the can, it was the red-and-silver Illy. But there were only some coins left in the can, and the bills were all gone. After that, I learned to never show anyone your money, unless you're ready to lose it.

The next morning, I was the first person at the bank. I canceled my Mastercard, forever, I didn't want to be in the credit game anymore. I showed my passport and withdrew the exact amount that was stolen with my wallet. I made it to the Manhattan CVS half an hour after opening and paid my debt to the homeless man and his dog. There was still plenty of time to go back to my apartment, still enough time for a CVS Retreat. It would take me three to four hours, about the average time it takes a New York lunatic to complete the marathon.

I filled the bathtub with hot water, adding soap, rosemary, two sticks of cinnamon, and a cup of extra-virgin olive oil. It was too hot, I would burn myself if I went in immediately, so in the meantime I flipped through the students' notebooks, counting them, making sure everybody was doing their reading and nobody's parents were getting a divorce.

The water was boiling, it made my skin itch. By the time I submerged myself my face was sweating. I soaked for a while, not moving, letting my flesh soften and absorb the aroma.

I then began to specialize, starting with a pedicure. I had everything ready in my new CVS basket, by my side. I removed my nail polish and dumped the red cotton balls in the water, I pushed back my cuticles and clipped them, I cut my nails as short as they would go and filed them. The tools went back in the basket, the waste in the water, which got gradually colder and murkier. I then shaved my entire body, using a new razor. I took a lot of breaks in between, the small room was steaming, my heart was beating faster than usual. I thought it was a bit like I was cooking myself in a soup, and I wondered if I should add more to it, maybe cardamom.

My phone rang, it was Curls. I dried my hands and picked up, my voice sounding strange in the small room filled with water. She wanted to confirm that I was coming to the gala. I told her again that I was bringing Sasha, I listened closely for the feeling in her voice, and I was relieved to hear none. I put the phone down but then it rang again, it was Sasha. I pretended for a moment that I had forgotten about the gala, to hear the feeling in his voice, then I abruptly hung up.

No, I'm not proud of how I treated him. And I eventually paid for it because I ended up alone.

I continued shaving, scrubbing, but I then remembered that Sasha had keys to my apartment, and I became scared that he would show up, that at first he would knock on the door and then he would use the keys I gave him, that he would see me like this. Sasha had seen more of me than anyone else, certainly since I had started showing up at his apartment after the garbage sorting, but never like this, never in the middle of a CVS Retreat. I jumped out of the bathtub, steaming in the cold air, and bolted the door.

Next was the Turkish hammam loofah, two snakes on my left arm, baby snakes on my belly, thick ones on my ass and thighs, I think from the days with Trenchcoat, he had distracted me. I held the snakes between my fingers and before I dumped them in the dirty water, I looked at them up close, looking for eyes.

They were what I was. They, and all that other stuff in the water. I washed my hair twice and rinsed my body while the bathwater drained. I stepped outside the bath, tiptoed to the sunny square, and looked at myself in the mirror.

I was flushed, clean. I had shed what needed to be shed, I saw it there at the bottom of the bath, covering the white enamel. At the end of the day, it was just garbage. But I had oiled and spiced it like it was a celebratory leg of lamb.

I t was a large production, with music, speeches, and a screen with a live feed of all the incoming contributions. I said before that I don't believe in organized charity, and what I meant was that I don't believe it can make a lasting difference. But I do think it's a good measure of commitment, and during the gala, I took Sasha's phone and kept donating by text, a few thousand at a time. I thought that if he wanted to be close to me, the least he could do was contribute to my people's liberation.

When they got to one million dollars, Sasha applauded as if he were hot-blooded, but I leaned over and told him that last week Chaim Saban alone had raised thirty-one million in Hollywood, and all of it went to the IDF. I'm not saying it's useless, I said. I think money is very important, but if we fight on this front, we are certain to lose. As I said this, I texted another thousand from his phone. It showed up on the screen under the name Sasha I love you. Pointing at the screen with my fork I told him, They have too much of an advantage over us, too much money, our only chance is to play by different rules. Sasha liked hearing me speak, especially when I was passionate or angry. He asked me if I was suggesting violence as the answer. They have that too, I answered, I don't know what our advantage is, I haven't found it yet.

We were seated at table number nine, named in honor of Bisan, which was my grandfather's birthplace. Bisan was now a low-income town in Israel, housing mostly Jewish families from Morocco and no Palestinians. Only a few of the original volcanic stone buildings remained, my grandfather's house demolished. Or so I'd heard, I had never been there, the place was too grim. Sasha knew that my family was from Bisan, I have no idea when I had told him or why, perhaps at that early lovers' stage when speaking of a deep tragedy brings you together and results in more meaningful sex. I knew his grandmother died in some camp, but for the life of me I could not remember where or why.

There were eight of us at the table, including Rawda and Curls, whom I didn't see until later in the night, she was too busy running around with her big nose and tits, showing lost men to their tables. Next to Sasha was a middle-aged woman, her hair dyed red, her husband next to her, digging into the main course, which was filet mignon. I gave her my first name, and she wanted to know where I was from. I lied to her and said I had grown up in Jordan. Sasha and Rawda both looked at me, they knew that I was lying, but they let me go on. The woman asked me which family I was from and I gave her the surname of one of my childhood friends. I cut my steak into four large pieces, barely chewed before swallowing. I buttered my bread, then took Sasha's and buttered it too. She then asked if my mother's name was Nuha, that I looked identical to a Nuha she knew back in university. No, sorry, I said. I was smiling, but I had dropped my knife on the floor, and it had smeared butter on the side of Sasha's pants.

Sasha and I both ducked underneath the table. I got to the butter first, with my finger. Sasha asked if I was okay, and touched my calf, which I'm sure was the softest and smoothest thing he had ever touched. Nervous, I shoved the cold chunk of butter in his mouth, first violently, and then, to make him quiet, I did it again, sensually, and then I put it back in my mouth and told him, You can eat my pussy with butter tonight.

It was true. My mother's name was Nuha. Did you know that? I couldn't remember who else I had told.

I know now that Sasha truly loved me. I don't talk about him much, and if I do, then it is always madness speaking. When I say madness, I mean the worst part of me.

Yes, I agree, but this story is not about him. Sasha didn't talk to the red-haired woman for the rest of the dinner. I didn't talk to her either, I didn't want Sasha to overhear or get involved. He was too sharp, and his memory, whenever it came to me, was infallible. I was afraid that he would make connections that even I couldn't make, that he would remember things that I myself couldn't remember. For the rest of the dinner, I kept catching the woman's gaze. She was staring at me. Her husband was too. Together they had seen a ghost.

In the line for the toilets I saw Curls, she was wearing a slutty dress made from keffiyeh fabric, just as I had anticipated. It was a reckless outfit, the thin fabric sat sincerely on her ass, and she wore silver eyeshadow and thick mascara. In general she wore a lot of makeup and reminded me of the extravagant third-world women at the Hermès stores. She gave me a hug, her breasts were soft, and said she had dumped her cis boyfriend. I told her it was an impressive event but that I hated everybody. These beaded evening gowns, I said, do these women think they're Lebanese?

Rich Palestinians, she told me, rolling her eyes, in New York of all places, the world capital of support for Israel. I agreed with her, I said, The more contradictions in your life, the more complex your identity, the harder your soul, the more difficult it is to love and be loved. I don't want to be with similar people, I continued, if you rub many knotted strings together, they don't solve into a beautiful braid, they just become a big ugly mess.

Curls repeated everything I said loudly, laughing, she wasn't ashamed that the other women were looking at us. We went into the toilet stall together, then we took turns peeing, and then she offered me coke and I said yes, sealing the line with a sloppy kiss that tasted like chlorine. It was a harmless kiss, I mostly wanted a secret to keep from Sasha.

I left her in front of the bathroom mirror, she was applying some lip gloss. Myself, I could never look at my reflection, let alone touch up my beauty, in public. I thought it was unladylike and a sign of insecurity.

When I saw her again, she was standing near the man from our table. I joined them and pressed my waist against hers, but she pulled away and said, This is my father. His name was Salim, Texas Salim. He made himself seem really important, and I couldn't tell if it was by New York standards, which could have been anything and everything, or by Palestinian standards, which probably meant he owned a small chain of ethnic supermarkets. He asked me what I did, where I lived, what I had studied, where my family was, if Sasha and I were married, if I had children. I took his questions seriously but mostly I continued to lie. Then he brought it up again, he repeated, My god, how much you look like Nuha. I nodded and stared into his eyes, until his whiskey trembled. He was smiling at first, then his mouth melted into a grimace, and I myself had to look away. He told me that Nuha used to be his girlfriend in university and I looked very much like her.

Curls's mom then appeared from behind and told Salim to leave me alone. She doesn't know her, she said, leave the girl alone. She looked at me and said, Sorry, honey. But her pupils were dilating, they wouldn't stop, I thought her entire eyeball would be filled black. I took another sip of the champagne, the coke slid down my throat and awakened my gag reflex. Struggling to keep it down, I covered my mouth with the glass and walked away.

There are photos of my mother when she was my age. Not many, mostly in the wedding album where there is too much fabric and makeup to see her properly. But there is one photograph, she is standing in the kids' room in my grandmother's house, wearing a midi navy dress and high heels. Her face is glowing in the flash, her features pronounced, her lipstick framing a victorious smile. On the floor are more pairs of heels, ten at least. I had studied the photo growing up, every detail. My mother was fairer than me, her hair longer, her nose bigger, her face wider, her heels higher.

That evening, I kept my promise and let Sasha eat my pussy with butter. After the act was a return to bitterness, or maybe just a feeling of shame and regret. I put on my underwear, pulled my dress down, and rezipped it. What happened? he asked me. I thought you were having a good time. I did, it was great. I kissed him to make him shut up. Sasha was gluttonous, always struggling with his weight. I liked watching him devour me plus calories.

He asked me to stay the night at his apartment. But I needed my shower, my bleached sheets. I told him that I was happy with him, but money was not the answer, maybe what I needed was nature. He asked me if I was in love with Trenchcoat, and I told him it wasn't the case at all, that in fact we had broken up and he was no longer staying in my apartment. Sasha relaxed a bit, he let me leave. I walked home slowly, taking small steps. My hands around the back of my neck, my tailbone tucked down, to give the coin some space. My vagina was slippery, my inner thighs slid against each other, trailing a scent of butter from the dick tower to the corner of the locked park.

That night, I dreamed that I was trying to scream, I had something very important to say, but no voice. When I awoke, the words were still on the tip of my tongue. They seemed very important to me. I rolled violently out of bed, slammed my naked body on the hardwood floor, and lost consciousness. In the morning, I was sleeping in a vomit of finely chopped parsley, which in the hours of the night had turned black. My mouth was dry, and in my nose was something like clams in white wine. Next to me was the latest check from my brother, intended for the month of April. On it I had written the words, You swallowed it.

The next Monday, Lauren called me over. The cleaners found this, she said, then handed me my wallet. I only opened it to find your ID, she added. I grabbed the wallet, everything was there, except for the money. I knew how much had been inside, three thousand five hundred and two dollars. Anything missing? she asked. Yes, I said, around two hundred bucks. She said a cleaner had found it in my classroom, although it didn't make sense, my classroom was too clean for the cleaners. Which cleaner was it? I asked. Maria, she answered. Which one is Maria?

During lunch, I sat in Tompkins Square Park, I wanted to tan my face. There was no one there but me, the trees were completely bare. The playground was empty too, because it was very cold and the slides were made of metal. From where I was sitting, I could see the entrance to Franklin, the door opening and closing, mostly the staff going out for lunch. At some point, I saw the door opening, Sal stepped outside and picked up a delivery from a man on a scooter. He took several brown bags, and paid in cash, but the delivery man didn't leave. Next came Leonard, Ahmed, and Felix, all Dandies by now, and each boy picked up even more bags from the man.

When I walked back to school, I saw Sal again, without a coat, still carrying the bags. I called out to him but he didn't hear me, I saw him open one of the bins on the street, the big metal kind that nasty orange cats pop out of in cartoons, and put the brown paper bags inside. I started walking toward him. What are you doing? I asked. What's in those bags? Are you still going to strike? Sal saw me then and started running. I chased him and called, Come back here, you're not allowed to leave school premises. Before he got to the intersection, he slowed down, then stopped. What were you doing with the garbage? I asked. Nothing, he shouted, lifting his hands in the air, revealing a pair of silver cuff links, shimmering in the sun. I grabbed his wrist and we walked together back to Franklin. The cuff link was cold in my palm, maybe it was real silver. Class is starting, I told him, go inside and wash your hands. I pushed him into the building, a bit too hard, and followed after him. At the end of the day, I took all the trash home. I wanted to know what they were up to.

The trash bags from Franklin were piled in my kitchen. Kids produce a lot of garbage, and it took me two taxi trips to get all of it to Brooklyn. Late at night, after the Smoke Shop closed, I took them all downstairs to sort them in the street bins. I had posted a sign to the paper-recycling bin, PAPERS ONLY YOU FUCKING IGNORANTS, and indeed there was only paper in it, letters addressed to Sofia, as well as her sheet music.

First, I sorted through the paper from Franklin. Chemistry quizzes, scribbles, the Frank O'Hara copies, all the signs the students printed, as well as notes that they were passing in class. There was a note in Carl's red ink, Shoot me, with a reply in Ahmed's pencil, 9 mm or 45. There was a note in Reg's green marker asking if he could copy someone's history homework. There were a few that I didn't recognize, discussing sneakers.

Next, I went through Franklin's waste salads, separating plastic straws, wrappers, baby carrots, and Cheetos. Finally, I opened a black plastic trash bag, it smelled of truffles, and inside I found Sal's brown paper bags. I arranged them upright on the building stoop. I started with the first bag, it was full of containers, the boys were only ordering takeout. Calmly, I sorted through it. There was no food left, I put my face to the cardboard and plastic, smelling beef, mustard, eggs, anchovies, frying oil. It was in the seventh bag that I found the receipt, folded neatly inside an envelope. Three De Luxe truffle burgers with fries and Cokes, two Nouveau burgers with fries and Sprites, one Wagyu burger with foie gras and onion rings and a Coke, and, strangely, one Let Them Eat Burgers with fries and a Coke. I scanned the receipt quickly, jumping down to the total. At first I thought it was two hundred thirty-six dollars and eighteen cents, but in fact it was two thousand three hundred and sixty-one dollars and eighty cents. I looked at the receipt again, it was from a restaurant called Afterlife, somewhere on Sixtieth Street.

I was certain then that it was Sal who had stolen my money, and that he stupidly spent it on luxury burgers, cuff links, and maybe even sneakers. I couldn't blame him, fine food and clothing are very expensive, and they're infinitely more pleasurable than charity work. But boys like him should invest in their future. Lifestyle is important, but it's not enough. Look at Trenchcoat, he was still a hobo.

At five in the morning the garbage men came and the driver, his name was Stew, said they had never seen a set of bins so sorted. He told me the plastic is picked up by a private company once a week. The city pays them to take it, he told me, they're all mafia, all crooks. And the green, for the biowaste? I asked. The green goes with the rest, he said, biowaste or not. I thanked him for his service and said I would take care of the green bin myself.

After they left, I dragged the green bin around the corner, across the street, and pulled over by the locked park. I picked up handfuls of the organic waste, hurled it into the metal fence, some of it went through, and some of it bounced off onto the sidewalk.

That weekend, Sasha took me upstate, because I had asked him for more nature, less money. I let Sasha drive, I let Sasha cook, I made sure to eat less than him, I let him massage my back and more. That was the balance of power between us. Unlike with Trenchcoat, I had to bring very little to the table, and certainly less money.

I should have predicted this, but I didn't like the country house that Sasha chose. It belonged to other people, a mother, father, and children. There was nothing neutral about it. I couldn't be inside that home that belonged to someone else, with all their memorabilia and rain boots and careless clutter. It was like being inside that red scribble that wouldn't come off my bedroom door frame.

Sasha stayed inside, working on his laptop, cooking four meals a day. I spent the whole day outside, and if it hadn't been so cold I would have slept there too. It's not your fault, I called to him through the tree trunks, I like being outside. I didn't want him to feel guilty because I couldn't deal with his feelings.

It was the end of winter, the air was cold and heavy with oxygen. It was better than being inside the house, cleaner. The sun shone from behind the clouds, casting wiry shadows all around.

There were mountains in the distance and Sasha had said something about the Hudson, so I knew it was nearby, but I could not pin the location on the map, I didn't even know the shape of New York State. And frankly I didn't care. I knew by then that I was a settler, I would take and I would leave.

I walked into the woods. The ground was lifeless and wet from the snow, which during that weekend had melted entirely. The rocks were a dark gray, like ash, which was a color that I had never associated with nature, only with wool pants and city sidewalks, maybe because the rocks in Palestine were mostly red or white.

I heard nothing at all, and then water nearby. I followed the sound of the water until I found the creek, and I made myself a little camp by the water, with my blue yoga mat. I sat down, and the leaves softened underneath me, they must have fallen many months ago, but they were still there. The trunks stood bare, assured, unafraid of what had just happened to them. If I hadn't lived all my years, I would have never guessed that there was still life inside those trees. It was death, at its lowest and deepest point. The first signs of spring were not yet visible, they would only come after I returned to the city.

I lay down on the mat, time slowed down. There was nothing, not even birds, only water. I remembered that on the car radio, as we were driving up, it was reported that fifty-five people were killed in Gaza, and I felt a pinch in my chest. But when I looked up at the trees, at the sky, I saw that nothing was changed.

For a moment I felt like maybe I was cured. I closed my eyes, and slept.

When I woke up, I saw a deer, staring at me. He didn't move, he just looked at me. I had the feeling that he was curious about my presence, that he knew I'd come from far away. I moved very slowly, raised my head from the ground. The sun was still shining between the trees, I hadn't been sleeping for long. The deer was about my size, with almond-shaped eyes like mine. His contour was not still, he was breathing, and suddenly I became very afraid of him. I could smell him, his musk. He smelled like a good couch, like warm covers, a consoling murmur.

I looked back in the direction of the house, where I imagined Sasha doing the dishes. I began to feel scared, and I hoped that when I turned around again, the deer wouldn't be there. And then I became really scared, because he knew that I had come from far away. I was afraid that he would get closer, that he would chase me. I got up and I took a few steps in the direction of the house, then looked back at him, and he only blinked. I started walking faster, then running, I made it to the steps of the back porch. I could see Sasha inside and I called his name.

For months I had complained to Sasha that I was suffering because there was no nature in New York. And then just outside the city, I found real wilderness. I knew it as soon as I stepped out of the car. The trees were the tallest I had ever seen. There were long stretches of undisturbed mountains, naked branches lining the horizon like the coarse hair of a beast. It was a kind of nature I was unfamiliar with.

I come from a land that is a graveyard. For millennia, all kinds of people were born there, they died there, or were killed, and some were even resurrected or reborn. It was bloody, haunted, and doomed, but it belonged to mankind. Nature in America was uncivilized and untamed. I didn't know how to read it. If a deer was some kind of warning sign, I wouldn't have known.

Before Sasha could see him, the deer turned around and left. I saw his fluffy white tail behind him, like the tail of a rabbit, and all my fear turned into giddiness. Sasha didn't leave the house to look for the deer, he stayed indoors, keeping a distance from nature. He was a complex man, but you have to understand that everything outside of me only serves a function.

Yes, I am a good woman, I respect people, I listen to their voices. Yours too. But this is not Bakhtin's carnival, this is a centralized nervous system.

On our second day upstate, the sun was blasting and the leftover snow had all melted, so I decided to take my clothes off to bathe in the creek. The water was too cold to submerge myself slowly like it was a CVS Retreat, so I counted to three and lay down at once. Remaining in the water, I counted to three again, ten times. I only count in Arabic. After that, I was good, my breathing slowed down.

The water ran along my boundaries, dead leaves and twigs tangled in my long hair. My back was stuck to the slimy creek bed. I found a sharp stone sticking out of the bedrock, I made it touch the coin.

And then I felt a sharp bite. On my wrist. A leech, the size of a beauty mark. I began to feel the same biting all over my body, my back, inside my thighs, a rushing of blood, as if I had been sleeping on a bed of spears. I thought, My backside is covered in leeches.

I looked all over, I felt around. It was still cold, the wind blew in my ears, my wet hair dripping like icicles down to my thighs. But there were no other leeches, only the one on my wrist. I looked at it, up close, it had no eyes, and when I looked back up, the deer was there again. He wagged his tail. He told me that I needed friends.

So I looked for them, the leeches. I looked around the rocks, flipped them, collected the biggest ones I could find. Some were black, others were yellow. A soggy twig whispered in my ear that I needed an even number. I already had one, and I settled on eleven more.

In my settlement on the blue yoga mat I attached them to my body. The first one on my right wrist, to match the left. Two on my ankles, two on the dimples of my lower back. They kept falling off, I had to take my time with each one, if it didn't like a place then I gave it another. I was very cold, I began to sneeze, my nipples hardened. Two leeches on my temples, and, finally, the four yellow ones, at each corner of the square.

The wind began to blow harder. The deer went home to have dinner with his family. I walked through the meadow, the yellow grass flattened unevenly in soft mounds. I walked like a nomad migrating through the great desert, leaving my footprints behind. By the time I made it to the pond I was dragging myself, I was so thirsty, the journey had been so long. I lowered my face to the water, I saw my reflection, my lips were dark purple. But I didn't drink it, I understood that it was not for drinking, that last time I drank of the primordial matter, in the bathtub before the gala, I vomited at night.

Inside the pond I floated for a long time, pools of black fish congregating around me. Some of the fish were golden, they were my good luck. I whispered to them my secret desires, I asked for help. I prayed to be healed. I said to myself, Nature is my medicine. I was immersed in the whistling of the trees, the branches animated by the wind. When a red robin flew over my head, a streak of my own red blood across the setting sky, I knew that was enough. I plucked the leeches off and put them back in the stream, carrying my clothes in my arms back to the house. My

Marni pants and the reclaimed-cashmere sweater by Stella McCartney, the queen of eco fashion.

Sasha had just poured the unoaked Chardonnay into the risotto. I took a long, hot shower upstairs. I cleaned myself thoroughly. I cut my hair like Cleopatra, straight bangs covering my eyebrows. I put on thick black eyeliner, clean clothes.

I came down and we had a nice dinner. I miss home, I told him. We talked about my mother, about what I had left behind. At one point he told me, You don't have to carry it with you everywhere you go. I thought he was talking about the coin so I just said, I'm not carrying it, it's sitting there between the grooves, frankly I think it's stuck. We made love too, twice that weekend. It sounds like a reconciliation but it was the last of us, a bright flash before extinction.

Jay told me that The Movement for Beauty and Justice had officially split, and Sal was leading the Beauty wing, whereas Leonard was leading Justice. I was sure then that it was Sal who had stolen my wallet, but I didn't say this to Aisha. In fact, I insinuated that it was Maria, the cleaner. I don't blame her for stealing my money, I told Aisha, I probably would have done the same if they were paying me eight dollars an hour and I came across a wallet made of red crocodile skin.

A few days later, Aisha called me in for a meeting. She started by saying, I've noticed some strange activity in your classroom. She said there were cameras all around Franklin, and she had seen what happened that Friday, the day that my wallet went missing. What do you mean? I asked. That Friday, she said, in the sixth-grade class, the students got up from their seats and started running and dancing around the room, and then they all lay down on the floor and the video frame barely moved for the remaining hour. I thought my computer had frozen, she said. Were you sleeping? I laughed, confessing that I had given them a special activity. They're stressed, I said, they're just kids, for fuck's sake, plus I gave them a lot of homework over the weekend.

As I was talking, Aisha opened her laptop, plugged in a USB

drive. While the computer loaded, she flipped a piece of paper on her desk. Did you see this? she asked me, turning the page so I could read it. It was the letter threatening to go on strike, printed. Yes, I laughed, it's everywhere, in the hallways too. No, they crossed a line, she said, let me show you. There was only one file on the drive, a video. It happened at the end of the day, she said, then played the clip. It was sixteen seconds long, taken from the angle of the windows, as if you were looking into my classroom from First Avenue, from the point of view of the fish tank. My desk was on the left side of the screen, and there I was. I am wearing my Gucci shirt that is very tight, I am leaning on my desk, my back arched like a bow. Reg, Ahmed, and Sal are standing in front of me, and I'm talking to them, my hands are moving fast, and I am laughing but they're not. I then turn my head to the door and exit the classroom. The boys follow me with their backpacks, it's the end of the day, the time stamp is 14:50. For a few seconds, the classroom is empty. Then a big head appears from the bottom of the screen, near the windows. It's Leonard's head. The door of the classroom closes, spontaneously. Leonard approaches my desk, his backpack in one hand and his notebook in the other. He dips behind the desk, two seconds go by, he straightens up, puts something red in his backpack, and exits the classroom. Another second goes by, the frame is empty, and then I enter the classroom with Jay.

Play it again, I told her. After the third replay I looked up at her and said, It doesn't make sense. Aisha remained sober, unemotional, she kept pressing pause and play, pointing at the red thing, saying, There's your wallet. I'm sorry, she said, but we will most likely have to expel him. She had already informed his parents, they were supposed to arrive any minute now. Aisha looked tired and disappointed, but then I saw a brief spark of anger in her and she said, This will put an end to their nonsense. They want justice, they'll get justice.

While we waited for Leonard's parents, Gregory went into the staff bathroom, for a long time. I thought that maybe he was composing himself in there, but when he came out he closed the door behind him, stood next to us, crossed his arms, and I could smell the bathroom on him, I felt that he had taken a shit. So it wasn't Maria after all, he said. No, I answered, it was Leonard. Gregory grunted, said, You can't trust these kids, then put on his backpack and went home.

It was already half past four, Lauren left too. I looked at Aisha, she was wearing a yellow print dress with cut-out shoulders and a high neck. She rarely wore the same thing twice, and I usually admired that she wasn't ashamed of her curves, but in that moment I looked at her and I just thought she was fat.

What are you going to do, I asked, are you going to expel Leonard? He was already accepted at St. Ignatius for next year, if we expel him he won't go, we'll be ruining his future.

Just then, Leonard's father came in. I'd never met him before, I'd only heard about him from Leonard, and read about him beating his mother, that he was unemployed and born again. I had imagined him to be an intimidating man, with a large watermelon head like Leonard's, but in fact he was short, bald, with no muscles, and much darker than Leonard. For a moment, I thought he was not his biological father, but then the man walked slowly toward me, shook my hand courteously, and looked at me. An intelligent glance and long lashes, they were Leonard's eyes. He was embarrassed, and Aisha convinced him to sit down. Please, Mr. Nelson, let's have a talk. I moved my chair, making room for him. He sat down and I introduced myself and told him that his son was one of my best students, if not my very best, and that if it were up to me, he would get a warning and we would all forget about it.

Are you sure he stole it? he asked. Aisha answered yes. Leonard doesn't speak to me, he confessed, he hasn't for months now, if I'm in the room he won't speak at all. Mr. Nelson had clean nails and a golden wedding band, I couldn't imagine him doing what he did, throwing his wife down, getting on top of her, hitting her head against the kitchen floor. I want to make things right with Leonard, he continued, but I'm afraid that I started him on the wrong path, that it's too late now. Aisha nodded, contemplating. I looked at his small hands, and I wondered how they felt, if a slap from him would be crushing, or if I could defend myself if I needed to. After a long pause, he asked about the consequences. Gently Aisha answered that she had no choice but to expel Leonard, that the violation was too grave. He shook his head, like he was angry at himself.

Before he left, Mr. Nelson took out two hundred-dollar bills from his pocket and handed them to Aisha. In a low voice, he explained that Leonard had told his mother that he found the money in the street. Aisha handed them straight to me. I unfolded the bills, and, to my surprise, I saw the red scribbles. I had been marking all of my bills after withdrawing them from the bank, exactly because I wanted to see if they would come back to me. Until that moment, I didn't really believe that Leonard had stolen my money, I didn't believe that he would spend it on nonsense. But now I saw that he did steal it, that he spent most of it on burgers, and that he had also given some to his mother.

When Mr. Nelson left, I quickly exited behind him, telling Aisha that I was late for an appointment. I walked behind him on First Avenue, I wanted to tap him on the shoulder, to continue the conversation, to explain to him that it was my fault too. I waited for him to turn his head, to see me, or to stop at a light so I could catch up with him. But he just kept walking up First Avenue, for a long time.

had followed Mr. Nelson all the way to East Harlem and then suddenly he disappeared. I looked around for him, it was the end of First Avenue, there were the bridges leading to the Bronx, to Randall's Island, there were bodegas with oversized signs and crackheads standing outside, swaying in T-shirts in the cold. I looked for the nearest station, it was Harlem 125th Street, and jumped on the 6 train back to Brooklyn.

It had never happened to me before, but there were only Black men inside the train. The stops came and went and it was just us. I counted, there were sixteen men. It got warm, I took off my coat. I was wearing the Miu Miu pants with embellished buttons and my boots were very shiny. I could see my reflection in the window, against the little blue lights flashing by. These men could be my students, I thought, trying to calm myself down, I'm regularly in enclosed spaces with sixteen Black and brown boys, whenever Carl doesn't show up to school.

I suddenly became very aware of myself. What do they think of me, I wondered. Are they also seeing what I'm seeing, that there are sixteen Black men on the train and one woman who is beige with dark circles underneath her eyes? Or do they just see me as white? Of course they think I'm white, I thought, look at the trimming on these boots.

I had never been so aware of the color of my skin as I was in New York. I saw myself, at that moment, against a paint palette, and I was truly surprised. How could I see myself as one thing and be another?

At last, a white woman boarded the train, I thought she looked like Monica Lewinsky, her face reeking of joy. Maybe I am just projecting, I thought. Maybe no one noticed. What is it, racial paranoia, class paranoia, gender paranoia? A man then got up from the end of the car and sat across from me, for no reason. I thought he wanted a closer look, but he didn't look at me at all.

We got to Lenox Hill and the selection shuffled. Two middle-aged women sat next to me, carrying shopping bags from Bloomingdale's. I spread my legs open, so my vagina rubbed on the seat and my knee touched the paper bag.

From Friday night to Monday morning I didn't leave my apartment, except to sort the trash in the street. On Friday afternoon I went first to the grocery store, then to the CVS again, then to Home Depot. I bought everything needed for survival. I was convinced that the city was making me sick, and I wanted to leave but I loved my students too much, I wanted to go away but couldn't think of a place. My only solution was to bunker in my New York apartment, to create a new natural order.

Before I shut myself off I went to see Sasha, because now was the time to apologize. We'd had a big fight in the car driving back from our vacation, I told him I had no respect for him, because he had no respect for himself. He said he didn't care, he was waiting for me to realize that I had no one else in this world, and once I realized that, he said, I would begin to appreciate him.

At first he didn't want to open the door of his apartment, but it only took me a few sentences to melt his protective armor. He opened it, I smiled, but he just looked at me sadly. What do you want? he asked. Nothing, Sasha, just to say I'm sorry. I'm sorry too, but I don't want to be with you, he said. I don't want to either, I just want to apologize, and I want my key back. He didn't stop me when I turned away from the door, so I had to stay by my own volition. He asked how I was doing, I told him that I had found a solution, it was not a simple one. As you know, I said, This is a condition of inequality. I have a two-pronged approach, I said, I'm going to address the problem from both its ends, not only the weak need to get stronger, but, Sasha, something needs to die for the rebirth to happen.

What are you talking about? he asked. In cyclical situations, I explained, the weak can never get as strong as the right, you know. So I need to cut off the snake's head.

The snake of medicine, the snake of imperialism, what's wrong with you, don't you understand? The answer is not democracy, it's equal opportunity.

A clean slate, I needed to start from the beginning, from the roots.

The project began as soon as Sasha and I returned from upstate. At first, it was contained, it had borders, like the square of the canvas or page. The night we returned to the city, I moved the tables and chairs to the bathroom, and I didn't think much of it, I thought that at most I was birthing a new cleaning ritual. The week went by like this, and I still did not know why the living room was empty, and then Friday came, and I apologized to Sasha. After that, I was free. I could act on pure instinct.

I went to Home Depot and spent a lot of money there. I didn't know why or on what or how. I was driven by something stubborn and aggressive, and by the time I realized what I was doing it was already too late. When I came home with all of the supplies it was all the same, not a moment of hesitation. I walked around the perimeter of the room with a pencil, tracing my height on the walls. Everything above that line I painted blue. Not the Franklin blue, a lighter blue, the color of sky. This blue, too, is simple. Blue, in general, is a simple color, that is why it's so calming. Below the line, I painted the wall the color of sand. When I felt that it was beginning to dry, I started playing with it, with my palms, my feet, I gave it some texture. Then I nailed wooden lattices, which I had painted green, the color of the leaf of a lemon tree, on top of the sand. The exterior wall, the one facing Fulton Street and the bus stop, was the strategic border. I covered the windows with barbed wire and draped some torn plastic bags on top, as if they had been blown by the wind.

There was no bathroom. The bathroom is where it all started so I boarded it up. With wood and nails and a paper that said, STAY HOME TO SAVE LIVES.

In the center of the empty room I had, somehow, I can't remember the details, erected a big mound of dirt. It was a mixture, something between seven spice and the pile of ugly Vetements clothes at Saks. It was made up of potting soil, white sand, organic fertilizer, red and green clay, cumin, cinnamon, and gravel.

If I had been thinking about what I was doing, then the thought of having to clean up would have been enough to turn me away. For months I had tried to get a grip on things, control my surroundings and body. I was tired of shaving, I was tired of cleaning, I was tired of sanity. But I did not accept defeat. I kept adapting. Even at my lowest point, having realized that my strategy to impose order had failed bitterly, because one cannot fight against time, or the city, I had morphed again and invented a new way forward.

In those eight months, I felt that I had lived the evolution of living matter. Every day was an offshoot. If it had hit a border and died, a new one would grow elsewhere. If it had found a way through, it twisted and grew thicker. And I must tell you that sleep is very important. In a way, sleep was my closest ally, because it broke time apart. If my existence had been continuous, I wouldn't have made it.

What I'm telling you is a story of survival. It's important for you to know this, that I cannot be defeated, because sometimes I feel that you are testing me.

The project was to create a new natural order. The idea had come to me from the nature of upstate New York, and the greenhouse in Paris. But I understood that what I needed was different, something older, a regression to my biblical homeland. We were not farmers, my family was of the urban elite. In fact, my great-grandfather was a wealthy landowner. In 1948, the falahin who were working his fields became refugees and Israel confiscated all his land. He went from rich to poor and died of heartache in front of my grandmother. So what I know about nature, I know from her garden. Herbs, citrus, nuts, those wonderful fruits whose names probably don't exist in English.

One is like a pear-shaped apricot, with the thick skin of a grape that you want to peel with your front teeth, its insides wet and fragrant, with four elongated smooth seeds at the center, sensual like crystals but each encased in an edible placenta. One is like a blueberry grape but sour, it grew on the bush next to the lily pond. And one is the size of an apricot, the color and skin of a Honeycrisp apple, and the crunch of a raw green almond. The flavor perhaps a combination.

The fruit belongs to the land, not even to my grandmother.

You have to remember that she was demented by the end, she ate them without knowing their name, or her own.

Me, I don't have a name. I lost it in battle, like the knight who lost his shield.

installed with abandon, working from the bedroom, which was now the workshop. There was barbed wire, wild thyme, crates of citrus fruit, bags of dirt, duct tape, linoleum, wood and nails for the cross, a glue gun, a humidifier, a fan, and UV lights. Some things I bought and others I collected. I went to Fort Greene Park and collected stones. I climbed into the locked park across the street and uprooted one small tree and one bush, dragging them back to my apartment. I went briefly to Franklin to get the printer and the two fish. I even went to Whole Foods, for the persimmons.

The landscaping was based on my plants that had survived winter. I pushed the pile of dirt and spread it around. Layering, layering, layering. I must have lost thirty centimeters of my ceiling height. I planted the aloe vera at the center, the five vines in the kitchen, which I had covered in a camouflage wallpaper, not in dry browns like the American army, but deep greens like cypress trees. I placed the spider plants next to my bed, an herb garden by the windows, the ferns at the entrance of the land, the climbing plants around the wooden lattices and barbed wire. The remaining cacti I placed in a row, creating a new floor plan in the room, separating the sleeping area, which was the blue yoga mat, from the recreational area, which was a kiddie pool in the sunny square. I filled it with water, lilies, Beauty and Justice, and a fifteen-year-old koi I purchased in Chinatown.

For the bathroom, I made myself a litter box, a bucket that I painted with flowers and suns in acrylic pastels. I planted a lavender next to it, fragrant and serene. If I needed to go to the bathroom, I used one of my white towels, of which I had six in total, in different sizes. I would put a towel in the bucket, and after I finished, I layered it over with another towel. When the bucket was full, at the end of the day, I dumped it all in the washing machine. I told you already that this washing machine was shaped like a toilet bowl. I would run it once, on thirty. A second time, on sixty and with detergent. A third time, on ninety and with detergent and bleach. You wouldn't believe it, but the towels came out clean. I was giving up a lot of my old habits, I was giving up on the comforts of modernity, even on my clothes. But I was too attached to doing laundry, and I continued doing it, I just did it differently, I did it harder.

When I was little, I had a Jewish friend, a very gentle girl who dreamed of becoming a ballerina. She lived in a beautiful house with thick stone walls, arched windows, and a lush garden. It was the house of a Palestinian family that had been expelled in 1948, and her father was born there, a few years after the cleansing.

I used to go over to her house in the afternoons, and I loved it, I loved her family too, although she was an only child and there was something sad about how quiet the house always was, with classical music playing softly in the background. Her mother would make us pasta with béchamel sauce, two small bowls and two small spoons, their lifestyle and demeanor very minimal. I remember asking my mother to make me béchamel but she couldn't figure it out, she didn't have the patience for it.

I loved my friend's house but I knew that it was haunted. Even at a young age, I knew that there was a family out there in the world that was still holding on to the key.

No, I didn't know this intuitively. Each time my mom picked me up from the house she made a remark about it. Of course, the door had long been changed, it was a modern glass door with a keyhole fitting a small aluminum key, which my friend kept on a friendship bracelet. I remember that above the door they had garlic cloves hanging. My friend told me that it was there to ward off vampires, but I think, in truth, that it was to keep the spirit of the original inhabitants away.

We spent a lot of time in the garden, playing hopscotch, finding sticks, and one time we even tried building a tree house on the walnut. We climbed the stone wall to nail some planks into the tree, and a piece of the wall crumbled and fell on my friend's precious ballerina foot. Her mom panicked, she thought her daughter would never dance again, and she yelled at the father that they needed to renovate the house, it was over one hundred years old.

Sometime after that, I came to her house, but we were no longer allowed in the garden, so we played with her Polly Pocket. My friend said she had a secret, but I couldn't tell anyone. She told me that when the workers dug in the garden, they found two underground rooms. The first room, she told me, used to be the old toilet of the house, before there was sewage. It was the poop room, but it didn't smell bad anymore. Inside the poop room was a secret door, which was locked. Her father told the workers to leave. At night her parents went in there, they opened the secret door. It led to another chamber, at its center a big wooden chest full of treasures and gold.

I never spoke to her again. I never told my mom the story, but I was old enough to know right from wrong. My whole life, I kept thinking of that secret chamber off the shit room, the wooden chest inside, full of the silverware and gold of the family who thought they would return.

Before I came to New York, I was visiting my uncle, and one night I walked past that house, I'd felt magnetically pulled to it. I slowed down before reaching it. I couldn't remember exactly where it was but I knew that I would recognize it when I saw it. From the darkness emerged my friend's father, in pajamas and slippers, looking a hundred years old, no longer the agile young father who used to drive us around in the cute blue Polo. I said hello. It took him a moment, but he remembered me. I think he was happy to see me, but he looked deep in sorrow, in pain. We only exchanged a few words in the dark, he was shaking, said he had Parkinson's.

No, my apartment wasn't dirty. Nature is clean. It's civilization that's dirty. The first few days were great, of course. The set was immaculate. I had acquired the healthiest, freshest flora. I spent long hours landscaping, deciding which plants got along, which didn't. I took into consideration the light, the afternoon shadows. It was both an aesthetic and a pragmatic practice. I watered carefully, with my eyes closed, like I was rain. The result was magnificent, it was warm inside, twenty-five degrees Celsius, and the humidifier was working all day, with extracts of the sage and jasmine. The soundproofed windows were always fogged, bringing in soft light and none of the visual pollution.

I had a wonderful dream there, in my transformed apartment, or perhaps a memory. It was better than the dreams in which I'm flying, or speaking French, or sitting in Junot Diaz's lap, or playing the EGR Game but we're happily married with children.

In this dream, I am lying on the couch, and my father is sitting on the armchair across from me. I am a child in the dream, watching TV. It's a summer evening, the sun is setting slowly. I can hear my mom making noise in the kitchen and my brother must have been home too, in his room. I am watching an episode of *Power Rangers* and my dad is just sitting there, watching with me. The episode is very good, I watch it, enthralled, the yellow one was kidnapped and they were going to rescue her. My father and I talk a bit. He is the same age as when he died, the way I remember him, forty-three years old. He asks me how I'm feeling, if my ear is still hurting. I used to have a lot of ear infections as a child, I remember him dripping medicine into them, the salty liquid slipping into my mouth. It's better, I say, resting my hand underneath my ear, watching the TV screen.

When I woke up, I could hear his voice, but after a few seconds I forgot it again. I expected my ear to be hurting, like in the dream, but it felt okay. I hadn't left the apartment, in fact the living room, in a few days. My body, inside as well as outside, was warm and moist. I was doing just fine. I was still alive.

renchcoat came back to help me. Can you imagine what a project it was? I couldn't have done it alone. I needed a man, someone who understood something about drilling, electricity. I let him do the dry work, and then when the time came for the organic matter he said he was no longer interested, he found it disturbing. When I showed him the koi, he nearly barfed. I'm from the hills, he said, the smell of water-life makes me nauseous. I remember now when we were in Paris, and I ordered oysters. He said that he was allergic, but I knew it wasn't true. He was disgusted. I think for the same reason that he wouldn't have sex with me.

I told him, I will stay here, you stay in the workshop, have my bed. But the next morning we fought again. I begged him, Come in and see, just for a minute. He walked in barefoot, his feet leaving soft prints in the earth. He walked past the working area, which was basically the printer, printing all day, it was also my music player. In the eating area, he stepped on a pebble or burr, of which I had added a handful. The day before, I had asked him to get me more bags of dirt, but he said, No, the bags are heavy, they're breaking my back. The pebble must have hit a sensitive spot because he suddenly got very irritated. Why don't you just go outside, he said. What do you mean? I asked. Have you been outside? It's a fucking war zone. And then he screamed at me, Then why don't you just go back to where you came from. I became emotional, I took it as a racial slur.

It was the end of us, of course. But before he left I asked him if he could take something out for me, there was a fish that had died. He went into the bedroom and came back with a small Gucci shopping bag. We had passed by the Gucci store next to the Trump Tower a few weeks beforehand, on one of our excursions. Me in my hat and him in his fake Rolex, his arm around my neck in ecstatic possession. We'd stopped to admire the storefront, a glass shelf displaying the new handbag collection, floral embroidery on leather. And then behind it, in bold letters, Liberté! Égalité! Sexualité! What heresy, I said, how could they do that to the revolution. And even worse, and I don't know if you realize this, but people were not sleeping with each other anymore, they were too scared, sex is a confrontation. Or as my favorite poet once said, In the night there is a violet hour unknown to others, in it I meet the lover's body and we listen to the voices from the other shore.

So I packed the hard fish corpse and a small bundle of dried flowers in the emerald Gucci bag. Farewell, my love.

Before leaving, Trenchcoat passed a hand over the bougainvillea, blooming in fuchsia, then tapped his index finger on a spike of the barbed wire. It was neither the jungle nor the palace court. In hindsight I can say that it was like my grandmother's garden, somewhere wounded and yet wildly alive.

had another dream about my father. This one could not have been a memory. My father and I were sitting in the living room, my mother was out at the supermarket. My brother was in his bedroom, listening to Michael Jackson. My father and I are watching TV again. My father is in his armchair, holding a wooden flute, the flute of a shepherd. My father is blowing meaningless sounds into the flute. They are showing the clip of Muhammad al-Durrah getting shot again and again. I don't want to watch the news anymore, I tell my father, so he turns it off and tells me just to listen to the flute. In the meantime, Michael Jackson is getting louder from my brother's room. It's that song where the glass breaks and the lion roars. When the chorus starts, my father magically starts playing along, Michael Jackson on the shepherd's flute. It sounds just wonderful, and I get up, and I begin dancing, and then I have an idea. And in my dream, this is a genius idea. I go to my bedroom and I open the drawer that's underneath my bed. In the drawer are sheets of musical notes, and I bring them back to my father in the living room. This is how I know that this is a dream and not a memory. My father could not read notes, he was a natural, the music was inside of him. But in my dream, he clears his throat, looks at the notes, and starts playing.

When I woke up from the dream, Sofia was playing her music. I got up, stretched, and had my breakfast, which was sheep's milk yogurt with honey and almonds. Lunch was lentils and chickpeas with more sheep's milk yogurt and some parsley, which was the first of my herbs to yellow. Dinner was fruit. It sounds like a lot but the portions were very small. In between, I worked, taking care of the environment, and also I danced and played. This new environment that I created, it was opening doors for me.

I t was possible to recreate there something I had read about, it's called wilderness suicide. Some people, wishing to die, just walk into the wilderness until it kills them. What a dignified way to kill yourself, and so courageous. Can you imagine what it's like? You wrestle with your survival instinct for days, maybe one day finding water, another day wishing to live again and forcing yourself to eat some leaves and bugs. Wilderness suicide was possible for me in that apartment. It was possible for me to test my will to live, to see if I could manage with just my creation.

Yes, you're right, I'm always exaggerating. It was domesticated nature, it was not true wilderness. The deli was so close I could have sleepwalked there if the animal in me had so wanted to live. A return to the wild was impossible at this stage of humanity, at this stage of my life, frankly. That's why I got the koi and not a snake.

I called in sick that week, then threw my phone into the closet and let it die by itself. There was no way to avoid fashion, so I settled on nudity. Just like everything is political, everything is fashion. Even if I were to wear jeans and a white T-shirt every day, it would still be something, a statement. The shirt would be made of a particular material, a cotton that grew somewhere on this globe, in one of the hemispheres. The jeans would have a certain cut, and a cut says a lot about a person. There is no such thing as basic, just as there is no such thing as normal.

So naturally, I decided to be naked. Naked, like nature was naked, like plants were naked, like the sky, the earth, the water. It didn't neutralize my education, my color, or my class, but it was something. Something shed. And I was alone, totally alone.

Trenchcoat never came back. He couldn't handle it, the smell, the way I had become, or rather the way I stopped becoming.

I think I got stronger in those days. Because of the manual labor, of course, gardening is a bitch, you need to have the core for it. But I also started moving in new ways, building new muscles. I started crawling, for example, it was just a way to get around. Or I would walk on all fours, or slither on my back.

In the beginning it was odd, because it was constantly there, my body. I would see my nipples from the corner of my eye, or brush my hand against my butt cheek or accidentally chafe my labia while getting up from the ground.

And I found myself to be constantly touching it. It felt nice, much nicer than touching clothes. Clothes don't feel like anything, unless they're made of fur or silk. But the skin, to feel it from both ends, what a pleasure. At first I was only touching with my palm, running it along my legs, feeling the new hair, which I was now allowing to grow, discovering it for the first time. Then I started touching myself with the back of my hand, along my chest, my stomach. And then touching the bottom of my feet to my calves, my feet to my thighs, my feet to my face.

I began to twist and bend and attach me to myself, wrapping my legs around one another, one arm from behind, my stomach to my knee, the other arm around my head, touching my ear. I would writhe like this, like a worm, and I discovered many comfortable combinations. I suppose that it was also an extension of the Cattier Method, because by then, after eight months of practice, not only could I touch every part of my body, but I could also feel texture with my forearms, with my thighs, with my stomach, with my face.

I don't know if what I'm telling you is true, but it's what I felt, that I was so safe in my natural order that I had gone into a state of hypersensitivity, like my body's borders were loose, not just spiritually but physically as well, and the boundary of my skin, the top layer, had expanded and lost its density.

I could taste and smell more subtle things. For example, I could sense the wind draft that was coming through one of the kitchen windows. During the day it smelled like the deli downstairs, something wholly unconnected to food, perhaps the smell of meat preservatives. At night the draft alternated, depending on the weather. If the day had been rainy, it would smell like the two and a half trees in the neighborhood were talking and this was the smell of their breath. If it was sunny and dry, I would get the smell of the underground. Sometimes I got the feeling that the train had just passed underneath and I could smell it, or if I heard the homeless man groaning outside, I'd smell his blanket. My body, too. It produced new smells, after so many years of Lys Méditeranée in my nose. I think I told you already, this perfume was so potent that it was almost violent.

Yes, sound too. There was mostly the printer and the washing machine. Sofia too continued to play, but her notes were fainter. Sometimes the silence was overbearing so I would produce my own sounds, stomping or tapping or shaking dry leaves. And I played with my voice. I'm not sure how to tell you about it, for some reason thinking about it makes me feel vulnerable. I had never really explored it before. I am tone deaf, just the thought of it makes me feel embarrassed. And I'm loud in bed but amnesiac about it, I can never remember what I've said. I don't know how to imitate politicians or foreign accents. My breathing was always shallow, my speaking voice, as far as I could tell, low and restrained.

When we were little, my brother and I played a game called telephone. We would bring our feet to our ears and speak to each other. We did this in our rooms, on the carpet in front of the TV, in the grass outside.

Those were happy years. We played in the garden a lot, especially with the water hose in the summer. My brother would spray water on the stone ground, it was the only way to step on it barefoot at midday. It was sizzling, within minutes the water would be warm, and bees would begin to surround us. My brother was afraid of them but I wasn't. I jumped around on the wet stones, between the bees, then rested my feet in the shade of the lemon tree. My brother one time told me that if you freeze bees they fall into a coma, and we devised a plan to capture and freeze them, then tie a string around their feet and domesticate them into our leashed pets. I brought out my butterfly net and started jumping around, trying to catch a bee, my brother cheering me on from underneath the lemon tree. At some point, I stepped on a bee, it stung me, but I continued and eventually caught two. I put them in a plastic bottle, which we put in the freezer.

The bees did not survive. My foot got infected and swollen, and my father rubbed garlic on it. A lot of things happened to my body when I played outside, bites and infections and cuts and burns, but I always healed quickly.

Hello. Hello. It was dusk, we were on our backs, a few stars were twinkling in the sky, the call to prayer echoing around the city. My swollen foot was on my ear, smelling of garlic. The phone rang. Yes, speaking. My brother pretended to be the water company, asking for a meter reading. The phone rang again, it was my grandmother, wanting to speak to my mother then hanging up abruptly. Then it was my aunt, who talked endlessly. The pizza-delivery man, he couldn't find the address.

We had entire conversations like this, I loved the smell of my garlic feet, the dirt like breadcrumbs sticking to my cheek. It was like holding a seashell to my ear, hearing the gushing blood, the deep life inside of me. Sometimes I would play alone, bringing both feet to my ears, separating into two talking beings.

The days were getting longer, I watched the aloe vera plant grow so quickly that I sometimes wondered if it was thickening before my eyes or if my eyes were going into REM. The stalks were thick and juicy, I would snap them, carefully peel off the skin, and rub the wet flesh on my face. Sometimes I would grow impatient and just squeeze them between my fingers, my fists, until my hands were covered in the clear slime, which I would rub on my skin and hair. It sounds dirty but everything in there was mine. It was natural, I had chosen it.

I had experienced this raw physical energy before when dancing, or having sex, or sometimes just stretching in the Cattier Method. But now, in the new natural order, I found a different purpose for my body, a rejection of how I had used it for so long. I could put my face in the dirt, or eat on all fours. I could lie on my back and wiggle my legs in the air, then point my vagina at the sunlight. I didn't have a partner to play with, but I rediscovered my body's arousal and could masturbate for hours instead of just rubbing my clit for five minutes to the forceful replaying of pornographic images in my head.

A lot of boundaries were now gone, and the compartmentalization of the body stopped making sense. There was no more head, shoulders, knees, and toes. And at the same time, I realized that I wasn't going to morph into one mass. I could always undo the knot and stand up on my feet and assume the standing posture of the *Homo sapiens*.

I was one with myself but also separate. I understood that if I could control my body, move an arm, a leg, my tongue, then it meant that we were one, made of the same. But I couldn't control it all, I couldn't control the breathing, the heart, the will to live. Parts of me had their own desires, their own moods and needs, their own voices. It took me time to address them, in the beginning I was only comfortable with the obvious. When I was hungry, I asked my stomach, Baby, what do you want. And often it would say lentils, or rice, or occasionally cabbage, because the intestines were chiming in. Or if my heart was aching then I would ask, Baby, what's missing. And it would say a man, a hug, a cry, an uncontrolled laughter. And I could make myself laugh, or I could make myself cry. If it wanted a hug, then I would hug myself, I would coil into a snake. And I couldn't give it the man that it wanted but I could imagine, and I had some great memories I could call up.

Sometimes my ears or my nose or some other sense would make a request and I would give into it, very lovingly. I would sing along with the printer or smell a flower or eat it and try to smell it through my mouth. And eventually, I became more and more confident that this was a safe method of living, that it would be impossible for me to hurt myself this way.

My body was harmless, it was not hostile, it wasn't trying to kill me. We wanted the same things and were the same. When I said to it, Baby what do you want, it never responded meanly, it never said, Fuck you who do you think you are. It was benign, innocent, sometimes I would yell at it, Why are you hurting me so much. This usually happened toward the end of the day, when pain would flare from the coin, I would get detached, and then suddenly very aggressive. And the stomach would try to come up with an explanation, but the back would say, I don't know, I don't know, I never meant to hurt you.

Yes, I needed to talk to the coin. Not the kneecaps, not the collarbone, they were fine. I needed to talk to that foreign object inside me. The small silver shekel. In my family, the curse was also the key.

Do you remember how when we first started talking you could barely say anything? It was mostly just me talking to myself, in all my confidence, a sick but self-assured woman. And only when I continued with my story did something soften, you could even say it was my vocal cords. Do you hear how low my voice is now? When we started I was practically screaming.

Yes, and your voice changed too. I think it took some time to get a word in. It was my own voice, but it sounded like a question. I could barely hear you at first.

One morning, someone knocked on the door, quite gently, I thought it was Sofia. I started whispering to myself, laughing. At first I wanted her to think that I was with someone, that I had family or friends. Then I decided that actually I really wanted to be left alone. I'd gotten good at playing with my voice so I started moaning, it sounded like I was very busy fucking someone, or perhaps like I was deranged. But there was another knock, this time very firm, ta ta ta, and then a voice announcing, Exterminator.

I got up from the ground, tiptoed to the door, and looked through the peephole. There was a man on the other side, with a pipe in his hand that was connected to his backpack. He left my door and moved on to Sofia's, who didn't answer either. I remembered then the sign near the mailboxes of my building, PEST CONTROL EVERY SECOND MONDAY OF THE MONTH, 10–12. I had never been home to receive the exterminator. We occupied different positions in the city.

I had another interruption that day, it was Sasha. I recognized his knocking and this time, out of respect for him, I stayed quiet. He left, I heard his heavy footsteps on the staircase and then watched him from my window, walking solemnly back to his dick.

I was happy alone, in the depths of my mind. There was no one to arouse my shame.

tried to hold on to it, but time insisted, and things began to rot. The smell was unbearable. I could not leave another dead fish in there, buried in a bed of leaves, also dead.

No, thank God it was not the koi. The koi survived. I gave him up for adoption, eventually. I put him in the community garden on Houston and Second. It was Beauty that died, and I tried to bury it in some dry leaves but it kept coming out and changing colors.

Even if I had succeeded in replicating nature in my New York apartment, eventually I would have to deal with the question of death. Fish die all the time, fruit falls off trees and rots, flowers wilt.

There was something else that I needed to deal with. Franklin, my students, and especially the eighth graders. I had been gone for nearly two weeks, playing sick, but it was April 14, the day of the strike, and I wanted to support my students.

I unboarded the bathroom that morning, took a shower, put on some clothes. I didn't look in the mirror, but I assumed I looked okay, perhaps just with bushy eyebrows and the shadow of a mustache. I exited my building and saw that my neighborhood had changed entirely. In the time that I was locked in my apartment, all the trees had grown leaves, the locked park was looking like a jungle. In the subway, girls were in dresses, legs smooth. I fantasized about what I would see when I got to Franklin, all The Dandies in sunglasses and megaphones, saying whatever they fucking wanted. I was going to take the megaphone and I was going to quit, in front of everyone, once and for all, motherfuckers.

But when I arrived at Franklin, there was a big yellow dumpster outside, in it the debris. I looked up and saw that the windows of the second floor were burnt. The detail I will never forget is the blue carpet charred and skinned. A big piece of it, the width of my classroom, where only weeks before the sixth graders had napped. The entire top floor of the school had been gutted, and with it my classroom.

There had been a flood at Franklin, and also a fire. It wasn't an accident, because all the faucets had been turned on. The students were notified and none had showed up at school, only me, because I had been locked in my apartment, off the grid, and I hadn't received any of the messages Aisha sent me.

She was standing by the dumpster, said she had been standing there for days. Where have you been? she asked, her eyes running over my face. Upstate, in nature, I said, I didn't have reception. She said the detective was looking for me, that in these cases it is often a student, a prank that gets out of hand, or revenge for something. Do you think it could have been Leonard? she asked. I looked back at the dumpster. Everything was in small pieces and unrecognizable.

Aisha pointed at my CVS basket, at the notebooks of my students, and demanded I hand them over. I was the teacher closest to the students, I knew more about their personal lives and secret desires than anyone else. I said, The notebooks are personal, it would be a betrayal to give them to you, I promised I would respect their privacy. You're not a counselor, she said. It's not a student, I answered, I promise you it's not a student. I know them, they're all cowards. Have you even talked to them, Aisha? The only student you ever talk to is Sal, and he's not like the rest, he's different. They don't even have a sense of humor anymore. We've choked their sense of humor with these ties, they all slouch underneath their backpacks, if they laughed their ribs would break. Honey, you have to let go, she said to me. Go home, get better.

I looked at it again, the blue carpet skinned and charred. Then I passed her the handle of the CVS basket.

I went back home, empty-handed. In the late morning the train was still full. Who were all these people, I wondered. With no jobs to go to. I thought that I would enter my apartment and I would be comforted, but the magical landscape was no longer. The flowers were dying, the oranges were soft with patches of green fur. The fluffy layer of soil and seven spice had somehow lost its bounce.

isha didn't return any of my calls. I became very paranoid, and the only thing I could do to soothe myself was drink Chivas. I drank as much as I could, until I started growling, rubbing my naked back on the dirt floor. You were there again, I was talking to you but you weren't answering me. I told you the truth, why didn't you say anything?

I told you that it was all my fault. I had shown Jay my wallet. I told him that they could take as much money as they needed, because struggles need financing. I thought the boys would do something good with it, but they just spent it all on extortion burgers and cuff links.

It was heartbreaking.

Because I had failed to teach them right from wrong and, in another sense, because I wasn't who I thought I was.

You didn't console me either, and I just kept thinking of the burnt school, that they were going to know that it was my fault, that Officer Conley was going to knock on the door any minute now and see the condition in which I lived. That was it, it was me, it was the end of me. I writhed and growled on the dirt floor and stomped my feet on the walls in desperation.

I threw a real fit in the dirt. I started digging into it, like I was an animal, but there was a limit, I could not get to the core of it, there was no lava, just linoleum, and beneath that a hardwood floor, and beneath that an NYU student, watching *Gossip Girl* on her laptop.

I started sifting through the dirt, I had put some things in there, some loose change, a plastic fork, beer caps, a couple of rocks to make it feel familiar. When I found the rocks I got up from the ground and ran toward the strategic border. I threw a rock at the window. It didn't break, it just bounced off, almost hitting me. I really was Palestinian, I really was an animal. I did this again, over and over again, a couple of times I hit the wall, I also aimed at the skylight, at the sky, the clouds, the moon, which I was sure was behind it all. The rocks kept coming back at me, the apartment was armored. I kicked the printer then. I made a dream come true. I picked the thing up and smashed it on the ground, I swear I heard the fucking thing whimpering, and then I kicked it, over and over again, until my foot was blue and inky and bleeding.

I tried to drown myself in dirt but I only ended up eating it. I drank more Chivas, until I vomited. And then I committed the massacre. I killed them all, with a pair of Ikea scissors. I snapped them petal by petal, leaf by leaf, stem by stem, sometimes more than once. I peeled the rotten oranges with my long nails, I shredded their skins and smashed them against my body. I smashed the goldfish too, and yes I put it in my mouth, after I cut little holes in the kiddie pool, the water leaking onto the dirt, soaking my bed.

I wanted to be born again, and I tried setting the bush and cross on fire but they wouldn't light. So I broke the cross and snipped the bush with the sharp scissors until it was just a pile, minced. I chopped the roots too, and that's where I found the button. The Burberry button. The Burberry button with the green thread. I had snapped it off the trench coat, months ago, and chucked it out the window. I guess it had found its way into the locked park, into the roots of the bush, and then back to me. That's what it was all about. It was karma. It was spiritual, but also physical. Whatever you put out there in the world, it came back to you. It was a closed system, a reinforced planet. Garbage circulated, the same people kept showing up on the subway platform. We think the possibilities are endless but it's an illusion. The Federal Reserve keeps printing money, but otherwise there are a finite number of particles in this world. We are mortal, but matter is constant.

That's why I buried the Hermès bag, under the kiddie pool and the aloe vera, I wanted to know how long it would take it to decompose. I had stuffed the bag with organic fertilizer and a copy of my father's will, to expedite the rot. I wanted to know what would come out of it, if something would grow in its place or if that spot in the earth would remain barren forever.

Of course, nothing had happened, it had barely been a few weeks. I dug it out, the will was pretty much intact. The Birkin was soiled, I had ruined it, but the hardware was still shiny. I thought about metal then, and the landscape of my childhood, how it was saturated with coins. Roman coins, gold Abbasid coins, ancient Judean coins. There were shekels, mils, and drachmas. Emperors, gods, and queens. They didn't decompose. They just stayed there, in the ground. And the coin in my body, it was going to stay there, until I died, and long after.

I thought again about suicide, but suicide didn't think of me, it was a no-match, we were not compatible. I had a family, somewhere. And even if I didn't exist, they still did, like the joke about the chicken and the kernel.

Society accepts that people's suffering is equal, that I was entitled to suicide. But I was indebted to society, I needed to get better, and I had the means for therapy, medication, vacation, to quit my job and move to the coast of a third-world country, to fuck boys, drink palm wine, and eat pulpo.

Look, the only reason I can tell you all of this is because after I ate the dirt and chewed the life and vomited and cried and declared myself dead, I had the best, biggest, strongest orgasm of my life. It's always my sexuality that saves me, my truest and only pride. The thing that no pain, no brother, father, fucker, no fancy sadist nor whiny bitch can ever take away from me. And for that I am grateful every day, because I know that I am lucky, that it's not like this for everyone. Orgasm is dignity. I pissed myself in dignity.

I slept, for many hours. Every time I woke up, I forced myself to go back to sleep. Every time my eyes opened, I took a handful of dirt and ran it over my body.

Sasha never came back. Trenchcoat never came back either. He never came to save me. He disappeared, which I had always known he would. He stole some of my money, as well as a few items of clothing that he loved and that fit him well. Officer Conley didn't come either, he was a figment of my imagination. No one came, actually. It was just me. Me and my dirt in my apartment, day and night mixing, sleeping as a way of death, orgasming as a way of life, then orgasming as a way of death, and sleeping as a way of life.

You and I didn't talk after that. No, we didn't.

Ten days passed. I didn't say anything because I only ever talked when I needed to make sense of something wrong. I only talked to you in times of hardship. There are few accounts of the good days I've had, you will have no idea what I know about love, that I had a few friends who cared for me, that I have won medals and memorized jokes and have taken long walks in many cities thinking nothing of myself and only wondering about doorways, storefronts, human strangers behind fences and glass.

It's just the way it is, the oeuvre is deceiving. It paints a picture of misery, ambivalence, conflict. This is what worried me when the fire happened and they came looking for the notebooks. The word deceives.

Well, what story did you want me to tell you?

Nothing lasts forever. The stench became unbearable even for me, so I started cleaning up. As much of it as I could handle before going back to sleep. I scooped it in my hands and threw it out the window. The city is filthy, a handful at a time wasn't going to make a difference. Then when I could no longer bear the hunger I cleaned myself up, just to get the dirt off me, and opened the door for the delivery man. I started feeding myself, slowly cleaning up.

I thought I would have a ton of missed calls and messages, but there was barely anything. The same exact thing had happened to me after my four days in Cuba with Sasha. I called Aisha, I told her I'd been devastated by the fire. She said that she was too, that she hadn't left her bed in days. I realized I wasn't going to die, I simply wasn't. She was on the other side of the line, she asked me if they should buy square desks or rectangular ones like in the library downstairs. I said it didn't matter.

On the last morning, I was woken up by the garbage truck, because trash was now a part of me. You woke up with me, in the mornings you were always drowsy, slow to open your eyes. Hello, is anybody here. There was no answer, but a leaf on the other side of the room quivered. What do you want? I asked. My hamstring twitched. I answered, We're together, I'm with you and I'm not letting you go.

I had to go to work that day, there was no other option. Otherwise there would be no teacher and the kids would be running around the construction site wreaking havoc, and then lord knows what would happen, they would do badly on their PSATs and Carl would shoot himself in the head and Jay would clean up the pieces.

You'll come with me everywhere I go, I said to you, we have no choice. And then I heard a bird chirping outside, and I understood that it was your voice. And this is how we began to speak.

YASMIN ZAHER is a Palestinian journalist and writer born in Jerusalem. *The Coin* is her first novel.